M000032985

Cecil's Flighty Fancy

A novel by

Rhys Wolfe

Cecil's Flighty Fancy
Copyright ©2019 by Rhys Wolfe
All rights reserved

This is a work of fiction. Names, characters, places, and incidents are the product of the author's imagination or are used fictitiously. Any resemblance to actual persons, living or dead, or events is purely coincidental.

Cover art copyright ©2019 by Stef Szymanski Mates (tinyurl.com/stefmates)

Edited by Adriane Wolfe

ISBN: 9781670082718

DEDICATION

For my wife
Love of my life

CONTENTS

ACKNOWLEDGMENTS

I would like to acknowledge the following people:
Adriane, my manager and editor. The passion she has put into supporting this book has been phenomenal. Without her, this novel would not exist.
My parents, Ina and Rick, who raised and believed in me. Without them, this novel wouldn't exist, but in a different way.
All of my friends and family who have supported me in this endeavor.

CHAPTER 1

"Dude! Bro!" Travis exclaimed as he burst into my apartment on a warm San Diego evening. Nearly every evening in San Diego can be characterized as warm.

To say Travis is a dude bro is, I think, to say everything. For instance, there is his imposing size and musculature, and his spiked hair with frosted tips. Follow that up with his love of surfing and his love of his bulldog, Turkey. The times when he put Turkey on a surfboard, nudged him into a wave, and watched him glide majestically towards the shore were probably the happiest in his life. A more perfect dude bro you could not find.

"Hello, Travis," I said. "Don't bother knocking, come right in."

"Cess, bro, don't give me that. I got news, dude!"

I sat up on the couch I had been reclining on to give him my undivided attention. "Well, don't delay," I said. "Out with it."

He settled on an armchair, the largeness of his

frame almost overwhelming it. "So I was trying that online dating thing with the dumb name you've been doing."

"All Right Aphrodite? I think that's a marvelous name for such a service. Punchy, to the point, gives you the sense that those you meet will be of the caliber of the gods."

"Yeah man, I can't agree with any of that, but whatever. So, like, the thing I wanted to tell you is I got a date. It was easy! You should try maybe asking someone out instead of just sending shy notes back and forth forever. Also, you should tell me your girl's name. Anyway, the point is, I totally crushed it! Gimme some!" He leaned towards me and extended his right fist.

Instead of satisfying his urge for a fist bump, I furrowed my brow. I felt Travis's habit of deluging a conversation with so many barely connected thoughts should not go rewarded. There was some merit to his advice, though. I had been messaging a woman named Emily over All Right Aphrodite for several months, seeking just the right opportunity to suggest we meet. Perhaps, I thought, I should just give it a go and see what happens.

Not that I was going to give Travis the satisfaction of knowing I thought that. Thus, I left him hanging. His hand was like a lonely mountaineer desperately waiting for rescue, and my shoulder could be likened to the frigid slopes he was stranded on.

Travis grinned at me. "Okay, bro, I get it. I'm sorry. You could get all the dates you wanted. You're, like, the Duke of Dates, looking out on your kingdom for a lady dude to buy an ice cream for." Travis is one of those lucky few who can readily toss out a quip quick as lightning, whereas I must spend years to come up with one and then write it down in a book. He leaned back, looking entirely self-satisfied with his dumb joke. "Anyway, we're going to a concert tonight at The Casbah. The catch is, she wants to bring a friend, so I need my best bro to be a best bro and come along as wingman."

The prospect looked dim from my perspective. Blind dates just aren't my thing. I dreaded having to try to make small talk with an absolute stranger while Travis worked his sizable charms on whatever woman he had managed to attract. My only real choice was to decline his invitation.

"I don't know," I said. "I was thinking of just having a relaxing night in, and my roommate is making his world-famous *Enchiladas del Dia*, which I understand is a recipe passed down in his family for four generations. Perhaps next time?"

Travis was never one to readily accept refusal from me. It was his policy, I imagine, to wrestle any refusal I might give him into submission.

"Cess, bro, how long have we been friends?"

"I don't know, maybe a couple of years?"

"And do you know why we became friends?"

"Because you followed me home from the beach one day."

"No, it's because you're a bro."

I wrinkled my nose. "Travis, I'm not a bro. I'm the very opposite of a bro. If you were to put me into a room of bros, I would stand out like the least bro-ish sore thumb anyone had ever seen."

Travis shifted in his chair. "No, yeah, you're right, dude," he said. "You're not, like, a bro, anyone can see that. But you're a *bro*, you know? And bros don't let each other down, so I know you won't let me down. Are you letting me down, dude?"

"Here I am, slowly and gently lowering you to the ground," I said as I pantomimed the act.

"If you go, I'll buy all your drinks," Travis said.

I wouldn't ever want it said that Cecil Haverford was an unfeeling man made of stone. The Haverfords, in fact, take pride in their friendliness and willingness to help those in need. They also, as a rule, never turn down free drinks.

"Alright, I'll go along," I said. "I just need to write a note to James saying I'll miss dinner."

"Don't bother," Travis said. "The concert doesn't start until 9:00, which means we don't even need to be there until 10:30. We can eat here."

We enjoyed immensely the *Enchiladas del Dia* which my roommate, James, happily provided. He only complained two times about having to feed an extra person. James is the very spirit of generosity. Dinner conversation comprised mainly of him insisting, as he usually does, that the *Enchiladas del Dia* recipe wasn't passed down in his family at all but was a recipe he lifted from a Moosewood cookbook. I didn't believe him. Something that was so delicious could only be a secret family recipe; this story of a cookbook written by a moose struck me as rather thin.

Eventually it was time for me and Travis to leave. We bid farewell to James and slid out to the car.

The Casbah is near the airport in San Diego and is about the size of a sardine can. The stage is stuffed full of speakers and the dance floor holds about a hundred people in an area three people could comfortably dance in. A bar has been squeezed in off to the side, and there are even a few tables and chairs here and there for the aging rockers. The space is far too small for anything louder than a children's recorder recital. Reportedly, the soundproofing was put in because the airplanes coming in for a landing overhead complained of the noise. Needless to say, it was always packed.

The opening band had just finished when we arrived, and they were performing mysterious clean-up procedures. The dance floor crowd had dispersed as much as they could, given the tight space. Having the thought to get some liquids in me as soon as possible, I decided the bar should be our first stop.

"I suppose the place to look for your fine damsel is at the bar," I said. "Only natural she would cluster around there, right?"

Travis just grunted at that. He was being unusually taciturn, but he did make good on his promise to buy the drinks, so I had no complaints. He stood suckling at a beer, looking around with an expression on his face that resembled nervousness.

"So then, where do you suppose she would be?" I wondered aloud, trying to keep conversation flowing. "You can hardly see anyone with all the people milling around. You know, this reminds me of a time when I was still at UCLA. It was a lecture class and I was trying to find out where to turn… turn in…" My voice died away as I spotted a woman waving at us. I recognized her right away from the pictures I had seen, though to my mind they had not done her justice. The short, tight curls on her head were a lovely shade of red which I had never seen nature reproduce. Her clothes featured a garish combination of purple tights and a tartan skirt. "Good heavens," I exclaimed, "is that—"

"Emily!" Travis bellowed a touch too loud. I

looked at him in disbelief. How would he know her? As he went over and hugged her my mind was reeling. A number of farfetched possibilities arose in my mind. She was a sister he never told me about. They knew each other from a Tai Chi class they had taken when they were eight. They had plumbed the depths of an ancient ruin in some sand-filled land, escaping a succession of dangers and solving riddles each more mysterious than the last, and then decided when it was over to keep it strictly platonic. But I knew in my heart what had happened: we had been online dating the same woman, and while I had shuffled my feet and stammered my way through months of conversation, he had been making the bold, decisive action of asking her on a date behind my back. I felt boiling mad in an instant. Julius Caesar probably felt the same way when Brutus pulled a similar trick on him, though I can't imagine it stung half as much.

Travis led Emily back over. "Emily, this is my friend—"

"Cecil!" She cut him off. "Cecil, I can't believe it's you! I mean San Diego is such a big city, you never run into anyone here." She set off a laugh which nearly sent me diving for cover. It was as if someone had launched a cannon full of silverware towards a wind chime; tinkling and musical, to be sure, but loud.

I should mention a few basic facts about Emily that I had learned during our courtship. She was an art history major, previously having been a philosophy major, an English literature major, a psychology major, an Asian studies major, and a structural engineering major. "Well-rounded" might be a term you could use to describe her. "Indecisive" might be another. She moved here from somewhere in the frigid Northwest and still couldn't get used to there being no real seasons. When she wasn't attending classes, she made her living as a nanny.

I forget exactly what I said in reply. I imagine something to the effect of, "Ah, Emily, such a pleasure to finally make your acquaintance in person. I daresay you are looking positively lovely tonight."

"Oh my God, Cecil, I can't believe you actually talk like that!" Emily said.

My reply to her was "But of course, my lady. I am as honest as a certain Abe who retained the word as his moniker. Everything in my profile and the messages we exchanged is the absolute truth, unlike certain gentlemen who shall remain nameless." I cast a sidelong glance towards Travis, hoping my barb stung.

"One of my kids does that," she said. "Talks all fancy to seem like she's a grown up." She grinned at me. "Do you want to seem like a grown up, Cecil?"

"Certainly not."

Travis looked at Emily and then at me "Wait, is this that girl that you—"

"Oh yes, quite so," I interrupted before he could say something which would show me in a poor light. "Travis, you may not know this, but Emily and I have conversed for some time now through All Right Aphrodite." I decided that I should steer the conversation to my advantage. "She knows much about me, like the excellent copy I wrote recently for the Kitten Palace brand Cat Bungalow and Scratcher. *Enjoy your cat's life at the beach!*"

Travis scowled. "Yeah, no, that thing was, like, super lame. Also, that was three months ago and you haven't had a job since."

"My job is as a freelance writer and I continue

to retain it!" I said.

"Well I think it's sweet that you wrote something for a cat thing, even though I don't really get what it actually is." Emily said.

"Why thank you, Emily." I smoothed the vest I was wearing. "It's the best-selling item in cat furniture since the four-scratching-poster bed, no doubt in large part due to my writing. For instance, most people just state the dimensions, but I—"

"Emily, wasn't your friend coming?" Travis said, edging his way between us.

"She couldn't make it," Emily said. "She had a test to study for. Life of a student, right?"

"Yeah, that sucks. Hold on a sec, I gotta chat with Cess."

Travis practically dragged me to the other side of the bar. He turned to face me, his annoyance palpable.

"Bro, I think you should probably just go."

I looked at him with all the wounded innocence I could muster. "Is this really Travis I'm speaking to?" I asked. "I'm here because you asked me to be here. Is it my fault her friend didn't show up?"

"No, but now it's gonna be weird. Look, I'm sorry I asked Emily out before you did, but I think she's pretty cool, and you had, like, a year or whatever to man up and do it yourself. You did me a solid coming here, but Bro Code says that now you gotta leave."

I was about to object that he was once again using his dumb Bro Code just to get his own way, and furthermore, if Bro Code did apply in this case, then I would be the beneficiary of it, as a bro does not attempt to court the lady that his bro has already begun to court. But before I could marshal my thoughts, a voice which had been amplified to an earsplitting degree said, "I want to let you know that square inch for square inch, The Casbah is our favorite place to play. Square inch for square inch."

The band had taken the stage and began to let loose with a racket which would have filled a space roughly four times the size of The Casbah. No doubt the commencement of their set caused the hands of a pilot or two bringing a plane in for a landing to quiver in surprise.

Travis moved back towards Emily and together they squeezed onto the dance floor, which was already filled beyond capacity with undulating bodies and waving limbs. I remained at the bar for the moment to sulk. Then I decided sulking seemed childish, so I resolved to drink my sorrows away. The sorrows, however, proved to be more tenacious than anticipated. I decided a third drink was in order.

It seemed very unfair to me. Here I was, third wheel to a date between a friend, or perhaps you would even call him a loose acquaintance, and a woman whom I would consider the final word on womanhood, and I wasn't even successfully being a third wheel! That realization required a fourth drink.

Fate clearly had it out for me. Months of conversation, and now this. It appeared that once I dodged an arrow, here came a sling, and when the sling had been dealt with, outrageous fortune started being belligerent and another drink was clearly required. How was one to keep up with all this?

I was called from my thoughts by a promise from the band that improper dancing was at this very moment occurring somewhere in the vicinity of a street. I hadn't been feeling particularly festive, but I decided this was the sort of thing I could definitely get behind, so I wobbled my way towards the dance floor and lost myself in the revelry.

My memory understandably gets a bit hazy here, but I did remember holding a shouted conversation with Emily, shouting being the only way to be heard. I danced with her while the singer of the band did push-ups on stage. The swirl of the crowd then grasped me and hurled me about like a novice juggler with a chainsaw; awkwardly and with a lot of floor contact. I found myself dancing with about twelve other gentlemen, while at least three gentlemen who appeared to be Travis glared at me.

The last thing I can remember of that night is the band's singer looking straight at me, saying clearly and distinctly, "You're a caricature of yourself." And then, nothing.

CHAPTER 2

Anyone who has had a night like the one I just had will know that the last thing you need the next morning is your uncle blowing an air horn in your ear. Yet that is exactly what happened to me. I tumbled out of bed and did my best to glare at my Uncle Gerald. My head was pounding, which made glaring rough work, but I thought I managed it well.

"So, this is the state I find you in?" he said. "I'm incredibly disappointed."

"Uncle Gerald," I croaked. "Why are you here? Shouldn't you be running some bright young minds through the wringer about now?"

"I have a conference in San Diego and I wanted to drop something off to you while I was here."

I climbed back onto my bed, rubbed my eyes, and gave him a closer look. His severe business attire lent some evidence that he was not in fact just here to meddle with me, but I wasn't about to take his word on it without a signed affidavit.

Some personal history is in order at this point.

My parents passed away in a car crash while I was in college. It wasn't something I liked to talk about much. My Uncle Gerald, who also happens to be my Godfather, took it upon himself to guide me through the trials of life from that point on, becoming a constant thorn in my side. To make matters more awkward, I found it difficult to find gainful employment once I graduated from college. Who could have foreseen that an English Literature degree specializing in Old English epic poetry wouldn't be what employers were seeking? I ended up leaning on Uncle Gerald financially, who frankly had more money that he knew what to do with thanks to his husband, my Uncle Ted. Because of this I had to endure the occasional intrusion, whether I felt it was warranted or not.

"What is it you want to drop off?" I asked tensely. His presence was putting me on edge. With his thin neck and skin pulled taut across his face, he gave me the impression of one of those mummified remains stuffed into a suit. But more unnerving than that was the knowledge that he was almost certainly about to drop something red hot into my lap. I don't know how I knew this. Sometimes you get a portent, if portent is the word I mean, and this one almost certainly read doom for poor Cecil Haverford.

"You have a job interview this morning," he said. I was rocked to the core. I felt how one of those blind prophets must feel after they successfully predict an earthquake or tornado. Oracles, I think they're called. I'm almost certain that Beowulf encountered one, and if he was lucky, he was told to avoid his uncles at all costs.

"A what?" I shook my head, which turned out

to be a bad move. I made a note that sudden oscillations were to be avoided, flopped back onto the bed, and shut my eyes. "I have a job, thank you, and I quite enjoy it."

"Your 'job,' as you call it," I could hear the air quotes Uncle Gerald undoubtedly performed as he said this, "has made you approximately three thousand dollars in the last six months. Ted and I are tired of supporting you. I have arranged a job for you at a friend's law firm. This is your CV." He procured a binder from somewhere and tossed it on the bed next to me. "When you meet the interviewer, hand that to him. Please remember to remove the note with the address from the front. He will give you a few soft-ball questions. Answer 'yes, sir' to all of them. I trust you will be able to complete this simple task." He paused, then said, "I am disappointed in you. I don't want to be funding your hedonistic excesses. Either you get this job and support yourself, or you find the means to do so on your own. Do you understand me?"

He passed from the room without waiting for an answer, seeming much like the receding waters of a tsunami, and leaving only ruin in his wake, i.e. myself. I rolled over and looked at the sticky note on the cover of the binder. It said 10:00 am on it, along with an address. I picked up my phone to check the time. It was 8:30. I had no idea how Uncle Gerald managed to be up, about, and so far from LA so early in the morning. Then I noticed I had a text message, and my blood positively froze when I saw who it was from.

In college I had known a girl named Violet Andrews. She was actually a good friend of mine for some time, but we had an incident. In the olden times, it might have been politely referred to as being together without a chaperone. Modern terms would likely be far more descriptive. It will suffice for our purposes to call it an Indiscretion. And it was certainly a pleasant Indiscretion, with her showing a caring, nurturing side to her completely at odds with the severity she presented to the world. A single Indiscretion it remained, however, with no mention from either party of it afterwards. However, from then on, she tended to meddle with me much like my Uncle Gerald just did. Our friendship became rather awkward, what with her asking how I was doing, what I was planning to do after college, why didn't I study more, and a million other questions. Those questions may not sound bad to you, but then you didn't have Violet Andrews firing them at you. She moved to San Diego around the time I did, but life out of college being what it is, we kept in poor contact with each other.

I swallowed hard, suspecting the worst as I opened the message. It read exactly as follows: "sry i missed ur call, thx for the nice message were u drinking? lol call me later."

The content of the message is perfectly clear to me now, and perhaps it is to you as well, but that morning, with my head feeling like red-hot spikes had been lodged into it, all I saw was a swirl of letters. I did manage to get the impression that at some point the previous night I had called Violet, which had probably spurred her into a reply, such as it was. I decided to put it out of my mind. I knew I would have to reckon with this soon, but first there was the matter of the interview.

I gave a good hard look at the idea of snuggling back down into the blankets and skipping it. I examined the thought from every angle, but I knew this would end poorly. Uncle Gerald had made his position crystal clear, and I felt he really meant it this time. It seemed that the best course of action was to go and get it done with. Whatever resulted from getting this job, it was better than the alternative.

I corralled a stoic shirt and pants from the floor of my room, stuck my feet in a resolute sock or two, and grappled with a determined tie. Thus attired, I exited my room. James greeted me with a cheery hello, but I felt he deserved only a cold, austere eye.

"I'm making eggs and bacon," he said, not noticing the aforementioned eye.

"My Uncle Gerald was just here to see me," I stated flatly.

"Oh yeah, I let him in."

I nodded. "Just the thing I wanted to address. Did I not tell you to deny him admittance? Did I not say that he exists only to prevent happiness in all who encounter him?"

James gave me a serious look. "Cecil, your uncle is *the* Gerald Winters," he said. "I've read his book about fifteen times. I feel like he is my mentor, even though I've never had a real conversation with him. Of course I let him in."

I scoffed at this. James said bless you, and I said I was scoffing, not sneezing. "He's just a college professor, you know," I said. "A veritable demon in human clothing. I'm fairly certain they take an oath to cause as much suffering as possible."

"I'll ignore that because you're hung over and don't want to go get a job," he said, approaching with a plate. "I couldn't help but overhear. Me and everyone in the building, I think."

"Who even says I'm going to obey his

commands?" I muttered stubbornly.

"Well, you're dressed for a job interview, right?" He paused, looked at my disheveled appearance, then asked again with a different tone, "You are dressed for a job interview, right?"

I grunted in reply. He shrugged. "Have some breakfast and you'll feel much better," he said, handing me the plate.

I groaned. "My stomach is too much of a jumble to handle anything."

"Oh, I know of just the thing!" He busied himself in the kitchen for a moment, then returned with a glass of green, viscous liquid. It was about the foulest looking thing I had ever encountered. "Drink up," he told me.

"What in the world is this supposed to be?"

"It's a hangover cure. It helps with the stomach, cures a headache, and in general brightens your disposition. I know it doesn't look like much, but I hear it's guaranteed to work."

I shrugged. Anything that could improve the outlook of the day would be welcome, even if it had the look of an exotic, untraceable poison. I took the glass, had a healthy swallow, and made a wordless exclamation.

"Is it working?" James asked. "Do you feel like a new man?"

"I do not! What is this slop?"

"I read it in a book. The main character is out on the town, the next day he's feeling awful, and his butler brings him one of these to revive him. The raw egg is supposed to coat the stomach."

I felt my stomach violently churn. "The last thing I wanted this morning," I said severely, "was for raw egg to be coating my stomach. Who would even want a raw egg to coat the stomach? What's the purpose?"

James shrugged. "They always talk about it like it's a good thing. The raw egg is definitely the highlight of this cure." He smiled sheepishly at me. "Good thing you tried it before I did. Not that I'm hung over this morning, but, you know, for the future maybe. Did you know I'm interviewing for a job today also? It's at a law firm called Tompkins, Richards, and Armstrong. Are you interviewing at a law firm too?"

"I think it was something of that nature."

"Is yours downtown? Why don't we drive together?"

"I really don't think that's necessary. I mean, I wouldn't want to inhibit your mojo. It is mojo, isn't it?"

"I don't know what you mean, but let's just go together, okay?"

I let my mind wander as we rolled downtown, James supplying the appropriate amount of chatter. The whole idea of interviewing for a job of this nature nauseated me. Or perhaps that was the concoction which James had fed me. I felt I was an artist. To be locked up in a law office all day doing mundane, boring tasks was unbearable. It was clear that this was a waste of my talents and passion. Sure, it was fine for some people, like Uncle Ted. He could handle being a boring office worker. I had to admit he had freshened up some these days, but I remember as a child he was the wettest blanket you would ever meet. In addition, I shuddered to think about the amount of control this would give Uncle Gerald over my life. Working for a friend of his would give him all sorts of information about my comings and goings. Every time I had a bit of a night, the boss would know about it, which means he would know about it, and then I would hear about how he knows about it. It was not an ideal situation.

There was always the option of sabotage, I realized. Surely Uncle Gerald couldn't object if I told him I gave it my best try and came up empty. I had yet to meet the stuffy office worker who could stomach the idea of engaging me in long-term employment once I brought the full force of my personality to bear. I toyed with various conversation topics, but quickly abandoned that line of thought. This sort of planning wasn't my strong suit. I would just have to go in there, be myself, and get shown the door.

It was with a decidedly sunnier outlook that I parted ways with James, he to visit Tompkins, Richards, and Armstrong, and I to go wherever it was Uncle Gerald wanted me to go. I looked at the sticky note on the cover of the binder he had given me. The words "Law Office of Tompkins, Richards, and Armstrong" looked back at me. I blinked at the words. "What a coincidence," I said to myself.

The building housing the law firm was nothing special. Polished tile floors, fake marble something-or-others near the doorway, and a good amount of shiny metal things on the walls. No one decorated their buildings with anything genuine in San Diego, but they made sure the fake stuff looked fancy. I rode the elevator to the appropriate floor, stated my business to a receptionist, and got shown to a room filled with the sorts of people you would expect to be interviewing at a place with a name like Tompkins, Richards, and Armstrong. I spotted James right away. "Hello, James," I said as cheerily as I could muster. "Fancy meeting you here."

James gaped at me. "What are you doing here? Wait, don't tell me you're also applying for Junior Legal Counsel?"

"Not at all," I reassured him. "Uncle Gerald most likely chose a position of office assistant or some such thing."

He laughed. "I suppose so. I mean it's not like you're really qualified for more than that, right?"

I shot James a glare. Sometimes he could be annoying. One of the annoying things about James is his ability to efficiently do nearly everything. For instance, I'm certain he gets up immediately after his alarm goes off. No hitting the snooze button two or three or even four times. Another annoying thing was how impeccably dapper he looked. His sandy hair was neatly combed, his dark gray suit looked like it had just come from the cleaner's, and he even had a pocket square. But mostly I was annoyed at him calling out my lack of practical experience. Even though I didn't desire the job, I still liked to think I could get it if I tried. "Quite a number of people turned out, wouldn't you say?" I asked, changing the subject.

"I honestly didn't expect so many people here," he said. "I was really hoping that I'd be able to get this job and move on from where I am. But with so many people, the odds don't seem so good."

"And what is it you do currently?" I asked. I realized I didn't really know much about James, despite having lived together for some time. It's just one of those things, I think. You live with someone, share meals on occasion, give each other rides to job interviews and whatever else, but you don't really have those deep discussions.

"Oh, well, um." He gave his sheepish smile.

"I'm in a junior legal position at The Pet Store."

I said "Oh, ah," or something to that effect, remembering that he had told me this once before, when he said they needed someone quick to write up a little thing for the Kitten Palace brand Cat Bungalow and Scratcher. The Pet Store is a pretty big deal, despite the incredibly boring name. It's one of the biggest pet suppliers in the country and is based in San Diego. "Sorry, I guess I had forgotten."

"It's okay," he said. "And I remember you're a writer. Any hits since the cat scratcher thing?"

"You mean the Cat Bungalow and Scratcher? Well, that one was hard to top, so I've been taking a bit of time off to replenish my creative juices."

"And showing up to job interviews hung over," James said, not unfriendly, but perhaps a little bitter. "You're sure your uncle hasn't tried to get you more than an office assistant position?"

"No, there is simply no way. And no matter what position I actually am interviewing for, I expect I'll sabotage myself somehow or other. Frankly, what's making me nervous is the thought that I would actually succeed."

James seemed a bit taken aback at my blunt honesty, but then he smiled. "Well, that's at least one less person to worry about. Sorry if I seem a little bit on edge, I just really want this to go well."

"I'm sure it will," I said. "I mean, it even looks like you've been writing down potential questions and answers to them in that notebook of yours. I doubt there's a single person more qualified to be a Junior Prognosti-lawyer than you."

"Cecil, whatever you just said clearly is not a thing."

At that moment a man entered the room and asked for a Mr. Marshall.

"That's me," James said. He waved at me. "Good luck not getting the job."

"Good luck to you as well," I said.

With James gone, the waiting was much more difficult. The people who looked like they would be interesting to speak to were all looking at their phones. The rest looked dull and drab to me, and I had no desire to suffer through a conversation with them while my head still felt like it was being drilled into and my stomach was finding new and more interesting knots to tie itself in. Also those people were looking at their phones too.

The lack of distraction caused me to focus on the symptoms of my head and stomach all the more. The drilling turned into a full excavation, while my stomach gave up the knot tying and began to heave about like a belligerent rhinoceros. To make matters worse, nervousness started to set in. I cannot be in an office for very long before I break out into a sweat and my limbs turn into limp noodles.

When the man finally came in asking for Mr. Haverford, I felt like a complete wreck. My legs supported me about as well as a pair of soggy baguettes, and my spine wilted like a spring flower on a hot summer day. I gripped the binder Uncle Gerald had given me and followed as best as I could.

I was led to an office which one would politely call Spartan while secretly thinking that whoever resides in it must be the most soulless husk of a human being ever to lurch forth from wherever it is such soulless husks lurch from. The room contained an empty expanse of floor, a desk, and an overweight man. I don't think there was so much as a piece of paper or even a pen on the desk. I didn't even see a chair for me to sit on. My nervousness ratcheted itself up some more.

The man made a sort of grumping noise as he caught sight of me. "And you are…" he said, flipping through a binder which he procured from seemingly nowhere.

"Cecil Haverford," I offered. I noticed I suddenly did not have the binder Uncle Gerald had given me, and wondered where it went.

He gave me a curious glance and peeled a sticky note from the cover of the binder. "Yes, I see that. My name is Robert Updike. You may call me Mr. Updike. I am head of HR at Tompkins, Richards, and Armstrong. It is very unusual for me to be conducting an initial interview, but I understand you have a letter of reference from Mr. Winters."

I gaped at him a bit before I remembered that Winters was Uncle Gerald's last name. "Oh, right, yes sir," I said meekly.

Mr. Updike—to me anyway, perhaps to his close acquaintances he is Robert, or Rob, or maybe even Bobby—whatever anyone actually called him, he glanced through the binder some more before sticking me with his beady-eyed gaze. "Mr. Haverford," he pronounced my name with a peculiar emphasis. "What is it that interests you about the position of Junior Legal Counsel here at Tompkins, Richards, and Armstrong?"

I goggled at him and choked, feeling a strange acidic sensation in my throat. I recognized the job title as the one James was applying for. I personally would give my right arm to avoid it, but to each their own. I had assumed that I wouldn't need to prepare for this at all, that our discussion would be a light, breezy affair and we would part with the mutual agreement that I just wasn't a good fit for the position. Instead I found that we were right in the thick of it, with Robert Updike asking me the cutting, technical questions of the legal profession and expecting answers to them. Somehow or other my Uncle Gerald's advice on how I should answer any and all questions rose to the top of my mind. "Yes sir," I said.

"Excuse me, perhaps I didn't hear you correctly. Did you just say, 'yes sir' to me?"

A strange saltwater taste came into my mouth. "I, well, that is to say, yes sir."

Robert Updike frowned at me like one of those statues of Zeus where he's feeling a bit grumpy about things and is considering whether he should start hurling lightning bolts now or if he should first chew out the fool who dared enter his office. "Why do you look like that?"

"My apologies, sir, that's just my face."

"No, you look like you're about to throw up."

I gulped. "I think that's because I am."

And I did.

CHAPTER 3

"You did what?" James asked as he convulsed with laughter.

After my display at Tompkins, Richards, and Armstrong I had been thrown out on my ear, which was to be expected. James and I were now seated at a diner in University City, located outside UCSD, roughly 20 minutes' drive north of downtown. Diners don't exist in downtown San Diego to my knowledge, but I managed to convince James that diner food was just the thing to reward ourselves for completing our interviews.

"You should have seen him," I said. "He looked something like a ripe tomato about to burst. I really think I gave him a brand-new experience. And did you know Uncle Gerald actually did have the gall to set me up for Little Lawyer Constable? I suppose that is no longer an option. But if I'm to be honest, I rather worry about the whole incident. I expect I'll be hearing from my uncle soon."

James laughed again. "Well, no offense, but I

am glad you ruined your chances so thoroughly. My interview didn't exactly go great either, though it was more conventional than yours." He sighed. "I don't know if I'll ever get out of corporate lawyering."

"What's so bad about it? Surely there are certain perks. Free cat food perhaps?"

"It's soul-crushing, that's what's wrong with it. I didn't go to law school so I could review patent documents describing how feathers are attached to sticks."

"Hmm, I see," I said. I confess that he had lost me on this instance. I hadn't a clue what he was talking about.

It must have shown on my face, for he waved a hand apologetically and said "Sorry, there's been a lawsuit I've had to work on lately. You'd think that would be pretty fun, but it's really not. It's just splitting hairs over this wording or that, you know? And my previous tasks haven't been much better. I guess I just dreamed of doing something great. I wanted to actually help people, and instead I'm stuck in this world of feathers, balls, and springs on sticks."

My heart bled for James. I was well aware of the conflict between doing what your heart desires and keeping the wolf away from the door. On the one hand, your life lacks that fulfillment which these days we are all seeking, while on the other hand you are eaten by a wolf. Fortunately, this was an area in which I was well versed. James could do no better than bringing his problem to me.

"James, I have thought long and hard about this very topic," I said. "I believe I have found the solution you seek. I, myself, have faced this problem head on, as you are no doubt aware, and my solution is this: get employment doing what you love!" I said this last bit with a flourish, nearly upsetting my cup of coffee. "It is the most important thing, after all, to love what you do," I concluded.

James looked at me blankly. "Cecil, that's what I'm trying to do. That's why I went to this job interview. Naturally I want to do what I love for a living, but first I need to find someone who will pay me for it." He grew more animated as he spoke, until he almost had his own incident with his coffee.

"Surely there is something that would bring fulfillment to your life. What about doing volunteer work on the weekends? I haven't done it myself, but I understand that places like libraries are always starving for some fresh meat to help out a bit here and there."

He laughed bitterly in reply. "If you haven't tried to volunteer anywhere, then it doesn't surprise me that you don't know just how difficult it is here. Even to just volunteer at the library you need to submit a full resume with references, and it only gets harder from there. And that's if a place is currently accepting volunteers. Initially, I thought they would just snap up anyone who came in looking for something to do, but I didn't even come close to making the cut. I can't imagine what sort of person they're looking for."

"I suppose all we can do is imagine," I said, contemplating how no one would want James to volunteer for them. He certainly seemed like a nice guy and he did dress with a dapper flair which appealed to the eye. It seemed unfair that he was wallowing in sadness, with his best prospects for happiness to either work at a soulless law office or volunteer at a library. I began to think that James would be miserable no matter what his job was, having gone into the legal profession, and that joy for him was to be found in other aspects of his life. For instance, I don't think I had ever heard of him going on a date.

I pounded the table as a realization came to me, startling James. I had all but forgotten about Violet's text message. I would need to give some sort of response to her, and when I did, I would need to have a reason I got in touch. I now found that fortune had blessed me with not only a reason, but also an opportunity to help a friend, or a roommate at least, take his mind off the serious things in life and do something enjoyable.

"You know James," I said, "I happen to know a young lady named Violet who would unquestionably be interested in meeting a fine fellow such as yourself. What if I were to put you into contact with each other and let nature take its course?"

Law school was apparently a good investment, as his steel trap of a mind caught my gist immediately. "You don't mean a blind date?" he groaned.

"Absolutely! Think of this as the beginning of the rest of your life. Or rather," I corrected myself, seeing his skeptical look, "think of it as a grand adventure. I think you're sorely in need of one. Would you really have all this concern over where to work if other aspects of your life were pleasant? A job, after all, is just what you do to get by. True contentment is to be found in your other pursuits."

"I thought you said it's the most important thing to love your job," he said, though I detected a hint of uncertainty in his voice. The call to adventure is difficult for anyone to resist, especially when said adventure involves romance with a member of their preferred sex. "I don't know," he said after a pause. "I don't even know anything about her. I like to at least meet someone before I go on a date, you know?"

"I assure you, there's no need for you to meet her. I mean, before the date. She and I have been friends for years. I can tell you anything you'd need to know. For instance, her eyes have an almost ethereal glow to them, like a pair of luminescent sapphires. You might even say that they dance with a spiritual fire, like little will-o-wisps on her face."

James seemed impressed by my words, carefully crafted as they were. There was still some doubt in his mind though. "Well, what about her personality? Do you think we'd get along?"

I knew this was coming, and I was prepared. The trick was to spin what I viewed as annoyances of Violet's character into something James would greatly enjoy. Thus, what I said to James was, "She greatly enjoys spirited, good natured debate. The kind of thing an obviously learned man such as yourself would really enjoy. Real conversation, you know, not the sort of how's-the-weather, here's-a-picture-of-my-dog nonsense you've no doubt experienced."

James hemmed and hawed a bit more, but in the end he agreed to give it a shot. "I guess I don't have anything to lose, and I haven't been on a date in quite a while."

I said I would set the whole thing up for him, and all he would have to do is be at a bar called Starlight by 9:00 pm tonight.

We got home a little after noon, and James left to put in his required time at the office. I braced myself, pulled my phone out, and located Violet in my contact list. It couldn't be avoided that I would have to speak with her, but at least I had a plan.

"Hello, this is Violet," her voice sounded in my ear after the phone had rung a few times.

"Good day, Violet. This is Cecil."

"Ah, I wasn't expecting to hear from you so soon. My lunch is almost over so I only have a minute. Your message said you needed to talk to me about something important. What is it?"

I was always a bit unnerved by how directly she said everything. There was no "How are you," or "It's been so long." She just got straight to the point. It made me feel like I was back in third grade, when Ms. Wallace would ask me as soon as I entered class why I hadn't done my homework again. I gulped as I collected my thoughts. "Yes, well, you see, as it happens, if you want to get straight to the heart of the matter, the fact is that the important thing to talk to you about is, well, quite important." I cleared my throat. "Violet, we've known each other for quite some time, and there are certain experiences which, in evidence of the whole breadth of experience, would be, if I were so bold to say, of a nature to give me insight into—"

"Haverford," She cut me off. "You're rambling. Spit it out already."

It's true that in the presence of Violet, or even when speaking to her on the phone, I sometimes rambled. A sharp admonition usually got my brain humming along nicely though, and I felt myself snap to after hearing her words. I stood up straight, feeling a calm come over me. This would either go amazingly or terribly, but I suddenly felt that the actual result wasn't important. "Violet, I found a man who I think would be great for you. I've arranged for you to meet him tonight at Starlight." My spine sagged as I worried if I might have been a bit too aggressive. "If that's all right."

"No, that's unacceptable," she said. "I don't need you trying to find romance for me. I'm focusing on my career now. Also, and most importantly, it's rude and presumptuous."

"You wouldn't even give it a chance? He might be a good, you know, what's the word? Networking?"

I don't know how such a thing is possible, but I actually heard her roll her eyes at this. Imagine a kind of grinding noise in your soul. That was what came across to me over the phone somehow. "Don't try to suddenly turn this into a professional opportunity. Is this really what you wanted to talk to me about?"

"I swear on my honor. You see, I happen to live with a charming, handsome, very well-dressed gentleman who is relatively new to the area and could use some social contact, and I immediately thought of you."

"I'm flattered," Violet said, and I thought I detected something in her voice that told me she was anything but flattered. "If he's so great, why don't you date him?"

Violet is yet another friend who is very good at ripostes like this. I thought it would be amazing if she and Travis got together and started a stand-up act. As I've said, I'm not blessed with such gifts myself. Given about four hours I could compose a reply to her jab which would annihilate her down to her very atom, but in the fast-paced give and take of telephone conversations I had nothing to offer, so I ignored it. "He's a lawyer so he'll be able to keep up with you in terms of brains, I have no doubt," I said. "Really, this is a sure thing and you would be doing me a great favor if you just met him."

"Why is it a favor to you?"

"See, that's to sort of give and take questioning a lawyer would appreciate!" I exclaimed, trying to hide my embarrassment at what I just said. I didn't need her thinking that showing up to this was a favor which she could collect on in the future. I just wanted to be done with this interaction.

"You're lying, of course," she said, and I gulped. "I doubt that you live with this guy. You were drunk when you left that message, so probably you met him on some dumb binge, and he is nothing like you claim. If he even exists, which is another possibility to keep in mind. I won't go to meet him, but I will go to meet you, which no doubt is what you really want." There was another certain something in her voice which I couldn't place, but it sent a shiver down my spine.

"Violet, I won't be there. My roommate James will be. This is the truth."

"We'll see about that," she said, and another shiver went through me. "You said Starlight? What time?"

I gave her the relevant details of time and place, described again who she would be meeting, suffered through another set of smug comments from her, and then we said our goodbyes.

After such a harrowing experience I needed something that would soothe me. Given the time of day and the lingering effects of the previous evening, alcohol was right out. I decided frozen yogurt would do instead, so I grabbed my keys, put my shoes back on, opened my apartment door to exit, and bumped into six feet and three inches of angry dude bro.

"C'mon bro, let's have a chat," Travis said as he manhandled me into one of the living room chairs.

"Glad to," I said, suddenly alarmed. Travis generally has the disposition of a lamb, but he is built along the lines of one of those Greek Adonis statues, so when his temper does flare up he can be quite intimidating. "I sense something troubles you. Please, let's hear it."

"Yeah, something troubles me," he said, emphasizing the word troubles, as if he felt it was a poor choice on my part. "It troubles me a lot. You know what it is troubling me? It's you, bro. You're troubling me."

"Okay, okay, so you are very angry at me. What for?"

"You messed up my date, dude. I can't believe you. You're supposed to be my best bro, and what did you do? You just threw Bro Code on the ground and took a dump on it."

"No need to be crass."

"Took a dump on it," he repeated. "Got a problem with that?"

"Yes, here is the problem," I said. "I'm not certain how I did that. You see, I don't remember much of last night."

"You were, like, a fly in my romance moves."

"In this analogy, are your romance moves soup?" I asked.

"No dude, they're my sweet dance moves I never got to show off because you were there being annoying."

"That's not so terrible, is it?" I asked, remembering what Travis's dancing looked like. He has always claimed he is a great dancer, but when I have seen him in the act it has invariably looked like an elephant having a seizure. I decided to choose my words carefully. "That was only a first date, after all. You should keep some, uh, allure for the future dates."

Travis scratched a thoughtful chin. "Maybe you're right. But that's not all! You also tried to make me look bad."

I gasped. "Travis, I would never!"

"You said I was a meat-headed baboon. You told her I should be ashamed that I was a dog walker." Travis looked at me with real pain in his eyes. "It hurt my feelings, bro."

I was ashamed of myself. I've heard before that all is fair in love and war, but it's a different matter when you have to face the person you have pulled a dirty deed on, whether you remember the deed or not. "I apologize, Travis. I was out of line. Clearly I was not adhering to your Bro Code."

"That's why I gotta ask you to start, you know, doing that thing you said. Ad-hoc or whatever. You need to back off Emily, you know?"

I goggled at him. "I have to what?"

"Stop looking at me like that, it's weird."

"I was goggling at you, and goggle at you I shall continue to do. First of all, the word is adhere. Say it with me: adhere. Second, why should I stay away? I am romantically interested in her as well."

"Bro Code, dude! I told you! Bro Code is there to keep things from getting weird between bros. It keeps stuff from happening that gets us all salty at each other. It's, like, the code dude. For bros."

I sighed. "Travis, this pains me more than you can know, but I simply will not acquiesce to such an unreasonable request."

He looked at me without understanding. "What?"

"The answer is no, my friend."

Travis reared himself up to full height, his anger coming back with full force. "Stay away from her," he commanded, "Or, or… I dunno dude, but it'll suck." With that he stormed out.

I sat limp for quite a while. I didn't want to cause Travis grief any more than he would want to cause it to me, but there are certain things that a person should not command of another. There was no way I was going to allow him to dictate who I could or could not date. There was a part of me that shook like a leaf at the thought of what he could actually do to me if he found out I was with Emily. I thought on the whole it was better to lay low for a while. I would exchange a few emails with her, maybe make plans to meet up again in a month or so, after all this had blown over. Probably he would forgive and forget by that time, and then I would be free to pursue my relationship with Emily as I pleased.

I must have dozed off as I pondered this, for the next thing I was aware of was a knocking at the front door. I staggered over and opened it.

"Hi Cecil!" Emily said cheerfully. "I'm here for our date." She took in the rumpled outfit which I had slept the entire afternoon in. "Um, you're not going dressed like that, are you?"

CHAPTER 4

"Our… our date," I stammered. "I definitely remembered about that."

"It's okay if you're, um, busy," Emily said uncertainly. I must have looked absolutely horrific.

"No, not at all. Just give me a second to change." I ran to my bedroom and grabbed some fresh clothes. "Could you remind me again where it is we were going?" I called to her. "I've been asleep all afternoon, and I'm still a little groggy."

"You told me to meet you here a little before 9:00 so we could go to Starlight," she called back. "Is it alright if I come in?"

"Yes, I'm so sorry!" I cursed myself for my lack of courtesy while I tried to get a handle on the situation. It seemed like absolutely horrible luck that on the very same day Travis threatened me with undefined horrors if I should continue associating with Emily, she popped up out of nowhere saying we have a date. On the other hand, having a date with Emily was a good thing.

There were other aspects to this matter also, I realized. Starlight is my favorite bar in San Diego, so it made sense that I would want to take Emily there. But I had also told James and Violet to meet there, which made things tricky. I wanted to avoid running into Violet since she had suspicions that I was trying to meet her myself, but with how small Starlight was, I didn't think it would be possible to avoid her. The complications swirled through my head as I yanked on some clothes and pushed my feet into a few shoes. "Okay, all ready," I said as I exited my bedroom.

Emily was standing awkwardly in the middle of the living room. "Really, we don't have to go if this isn't a good time."

"No, no, this is good, really. Let's go," I smiled at her.

Starlight isn't much to look at from the outside, and it can be difficult to find, placed between the freeway and a residential neighborhood, but the interior makes up for both those deficiencies. Rustic stonework covered the walls, the booth cushions were made of dark leather, and small lights hung over the wood-paneled bar, twinkling like, and I will be a bit cliché here, star light. They served some rather decent food there, along with the best Moscow Mules in the city. When Emily and I arrived, fully half the people milling about had copper mugs.

"Wow, this is pretty nice," Emily said, seeming genuinely impressed.

"Yes, quite," I said automatically, my attention elsewhere. I had spotted James over by the bar. "Let's adjourn to the bar in the back. The seating is better there."

There is a curious question as to why so many

bars, lounges, and venues in San Diego have a two-bar set up. I formed the opinion then, and I still maintain it to this day, it is so a person who has set up a couple of friends on a blind date can take their surprise date to the same location without interacting with them. If you have never found yourself in this situation, the two-bar set up has no doubt befuddled you for ages. Now you have the answer. The point is, it was certainly advantageous that there were in fact two bars. Emily and I had gotten ourselves settled at a table when I felt a tap on the shoulder and a voice said "Cecil! I wasn't expecting to see you here. We could have carpooled if I knew."

I nearly jumped out of my skin. "James!" I hissed. "What the devil are you about?"

"What? I don't understand."

Emily let loose one of her laughs, producing a visible effect in James. "He talks really funny, doesn't he?" she said.

I gave them both a glare. "Really, who taps people on the shoulder? James, this is Emily. Emily, my roommate, James." The two exchanged hellos, James shyly and Emily energetically. "Emily and I are enjoying an evening out, sort of a last-minute thing."

"You invited me last night," Emily said with an edge of mock sweetness.

"That's cool. Violet should be here any minute, right?" James said to me. "Should we join you two?"

"No!" I cried. James looked surprised and slightly wounded, while Emily placed her chin in her hand and peered at me with a small smile. "I mean, it's the first time you are meeting. You don't want me getting in your way. Why don't you go back to the front and meet her there?"

"I guess I had better, I don't want to miss her," James said. "Eyes like sapphires, right?"

"Absolutely," I said, feeling very confident in my description. As he pushed off, I turned my attention back to Emily. "My apologies for that."

"Did you set him up on a date here when you were going to be here too?" She asked, chin still planted in her hand and the small smile still there. "Is it a blind date? Are we being spies?" Her smile turned into a Cheshire grin. "Maybe if it goes poorly I'll go comfort him."

"What? No, that won't be necessary. I just had a bit of a mix up. I've been rather disorganized lately."

"I know just the thing!" Emily set her purse on the table, a small toolbox with a shoulder strap attached. She rooted through it and after a moment pulled a book out. "I just started reading it, and I'm pretty far in," she said as she handed the book to me. "It's called *7 Habits of Highly Effective People*, and it's absolutely life changing!"

I glanced at the front and back of the book and flipped through some of the pages quickly. "Good golly, I think I'm cured." I placed the book on the table. "But now, Emily, since we are alone, let's talk about other matters. You're looking quite lovely to—"

"I'm going to the bathroom," she announced suddenly.

It is always off-putting when you are about to lay a red-hot compliment on someone and they up and leave. If Emily was less perfect in my mind, I would have held it against her. As it was, I said I would await her return. I watched her leave and saw her cross paths with the last person I wanted to see tonight, Violet Andrews. Her hair looked as blond and immaculate as ever. As she spotted me, smiled, and approached, I saw her eyes glimmer in a way that was nothing like sapphires because they were brown. A lustrous, luminous brown, to be sure. They were the kind of brown that brought to mind the pottery that sells for two hundred dollars in La Jolla shops. But definitely not blue. I immediately began to feel a tremor in my legs.

"It's funny," Violet said to me. "I came here expecting to find this mystery man you set me up with, and instead I find only you, sitting alone at a table. It's enough to make a person suspicious." The certain something was back in her voice and it sent a chill down my spine. She sounded like a cat with a mouse, if the cat was a highly intelligent, curvy blond and the mouse was yours truly. I gulped nervously.

"Oh, you mean you haven't seen James yet?" I asked. "He was waiting for you by the entrance. Perhaps you should go see if he's there."

Violet gave me a little grin as she prepared, undoubtedly, to tell me what she was going to do instead of that, but then her eye caught sight of something on the table. "Oh, Cecil!" she almost cooed. I looked down at what had grabbed her attention and saw the 7 Habits book still sitting in front of me.

"Oh, this?" I said. "You see, it's a funny story, I—"

"I can't believe it! You have no idea how proud of you I am. I had almost given up on you making an effort to improve yourself, but deep down I just knew you would get ambition sooner or later. Tell me, have you read Lean In?"

"Um, that wouldn't happen to be one of Rex Stout's, would it?"

She laughed. "Don't worry, I'll get you a copy." Her eyes shone with what I considered an unhealthy excitement. "I have to run to the restroom, but I'll be back, and then we can talk about your experiences with the book."

I put my head down on the table after she had left. This was about the worst possible result. Now that Violet thought I wanted to improve myself, whatever that meant, it was a sure bet she would not leave me alone for months. I was feeling about as low as I could possibly get when James approached. He was carrying a red concoction with raspberries in it. "What on earth is that?" I asked.

He looked at his drink. "I don't really know. I normally just have beer, but this sounded good. I guess it's kind of girly looking, but I like it."

I raised my head from the table. "Always get a Mule when you come here. A Kentucky Colonel is also acceptable. The important thing is the copper mug. Why aren't you with Violet?"

"Is she here?" he asked, surprised. "I haven't been able to find her."

"That's a bit difficult to believe," I sniffed. "I managed to locate her without moving from this spot. This place seems to be filled with nothing but Violet Andrews. I doubt whether you could swing a cat in here without hitting her. She said she was going to the restroom. Perhaps you should wait for her there."

"What and be that creepy guy waiting outside of the women's bathroom? No, I'll wait for her to come back here. I really think that since you and your girlfriend are here, we should have a double date."

"She's not my girlfriend," I said, resisting the urge to exaggerate. James nodded and made some sort of noise like, "Hmm, oh really," but I ignored him. The thought struck me that his suggestion might not be as bad as I had originally supposed. First, Violet had already found me, so the jig was up. Second, Emily would be able to set straight the notion that I had been reading the 7 Habits book by saying it was hers and she had just been telling me about it. Finally, James and Violet would actually be able to meet, and her attention could be firmly fastened on him. I said to James that perhaps he was right, and that we should do it as a double date after all.

"Great!" James exclaimed, looking relieved. "I'll be right back. I just have to go to the bathroom."

It seemed to me that restroom usage was at an all-time high and that the establishment might look into monetizing this aspect of their business. A moment or two later Emily returned, her curls bobbing, her clothes seeming even more mismatched than before, and giving the impression of a vision of loveliness greeting the worn traveler on his safe return. I felt a sense of relief with her back.

"Sorry that took a while," she said with the voice of an angel. "I had to poop."

I wrinkled my nose at that. I have a strong aversion to words like poop, especially on a first date. She was no less perfection for having used it, but I thought perhaps she should know of my preference. "There's no need to really say it though, is there?" I asked gently.

She shrugged. "It's a natural thing that everyone does. I don't see why we shouldn't be able to honestly say so to each other. Oh, that's where I left that," she said, spotting her 7 Habits book and putting it back in her toolbox.

I was about to say something on the subject of her loveliness when Violet suddenly appeared at the table again. "I'm sorry, I didn't realize you were here with someone, Cecil."

"I am, in fact. Violet, meet Emily." The two women exchanged hellos. "James should be here in a moment. We decided, since we are all here, we may as well make a party of it."

Violet nodded, not even missing a beat despite the mounting evidence that James really did exist and that she would soon see he was everything I said he was. With most people you might expect a small blush, or maybe a stammered apology, but not with Violet. "Sounds good to me," she said with all the coolness of a freshly picked cucumber. "Now, I just wanted to say to you about 7 Habits—"

"Oh, you're into 7 Habits too?" Emily practically squealed. "That's amazing! To think that I would find someone else who's into that. What is your opinion on the large stone philosophy?"

Violet looked surprised, but then the corner of her mouth twitched upwards, a sure sign that she was impressed. "Well, I could go on for hours about it. How did you discover this book?"

"A speaker came to my school and talked about it. How about you?"

"A work training. I thought it would be a bore, but it was incredibly informative and thought provoking."

I tried to take my chance here. "I just found out about it by—"

"Isn't it crazy how some people just don't get it?" Emily asked, ignoring me.

Violet nodded. "Definitely. Someone where I work said they had done the same job at the same place for the last fifteen years, and never felt they were given a choice. Isn't that incredible?"

"Yes! Exactly! Just doing that is the choice. Why don't people get it?"

"Speaking of choice—" I tried to get out, but James bumbled his way over just then. Thankfully he bumbled in a sort of dapper, well-dressed way which would probably catch Violet's eye.

"Hi, I'm James, are you Violet?" he said.

I saw Violet register surprise, a slight widening of the eyes, but she recovered herself quickly. "Hello James, nice to meet you. Have you read *7 Habits of Highly Effective People*? No? Too bad."

"I'm afraid we're about to be cut out of this conversation," I said to James. "Why don't you regale us with a tale about the charming Vermont town you're from?"

"Oh, sure." James considered for a moment. "So, there's this vegetarian restaurant there which is really good. I would eat there once in a while. One day some vegan friends of mine were complaining about how it's not a true vegan place. I think the word sellout might have been used. But that's not really what it's supposed to be. It's vegetarian. Why would anyone think it should be vegan, or get angry because it's not vegan enough? Just from that you can imagine the place I grew up."

Emily let out a little laugh. Violet looked at James blankly, then turned the look on me. Considering her point made, she shifted back to Emily. "Anyway, Emily, let me ask you this…"

"Cecil," James whispered in my ear while Violet and Emily went on with their conversation. "I thought you said her eyes were blue."

I had seen this coming, so I didn't have to bother with feeling like a trapped rat and just shook my head instead. "I distinctly said her eyes were like sapphires."

"Sapphires are blue, though."

"Yes, well her eyes would be like sapphires if they were blue."

"Are you sure you didn't mean Emily? Her eyes are blue."

I looked at Emily and, if you can believe it, James was absolutely right. Her eyes were a rather bright shade of blue and I had never noticed before. "Forget it, chum," I whispered. "She's spoken for."

"But I thought you said—"

"What kind of secrets are you guys telling?" Emily asked, a big grin on her face. James looked startled and guilty, in that order, and I'm sure I looked the same. "Seems like it was a good one."

"Don't you want to talk to us? Isn't this supposed to be a date?" Violet asked, looking down her nose at us. The corner of her mouth was twitched upward again, this time in a way that meant she thought she was being funny. She knew she was being a hypocrite, considering she had focused her attention solely on Emily since James had arrived, and to Violet that was the height of humor.

"My apologies," I said with a mock flourish. "Please, may we join in your conversation?"

Violet shrugged and turned back to Emily. "You had mentioned school. What are you studying?"

"Right now it's art history. I studied a lot of other stuff in the past. I just can't decide on anything, you know? But I think I've got it now. I'm really enjoying my program. What do you do?"

"Software development," Violet said.

"Wow!" Emily's eyes shone. "That's so cool!"

"It's not that cool." Violet rubbed her hair self-consciously. "They keep trying to push me into dealing with clients because I'm the only one with people skills, but I really just want to do the programming work."

"It's still really cool. I bet you're well respected. That's what I want someday."

"What do you want to do when you're done with school?" James asked.

Emily batted her lashes and smiled, and I fancied for the first time I noticed dimples on her cheeks. "Well, I guess ideally I would want to be a college professor."

"Excuse me!" I exclaimed, springing up as if someone had stuck me with a large needle. "I need to go to the restroom!"

CHAPTER 5

I sat at the beach the next day, enjoying the late-morning sun and pondering subjects including, but not limited to, love, fate, and narrow escapes.

On the topic of love, I felt I was pretty well set. Love was something that all humans should aspire to. It fed the soul, enriched the arts and sciences, and was downright pleasant. Love, in a word, was an A+.

Fate was trickier to me. If fate existed, it was both comforting and depressing that nothing could be avoided. The road was paved, so to speak, and we walked it enjoying the scenery. On the other hand, if there was no such thing as fate, we existed in a random and hostile universe, moving between success and failure by pure chance.

As for narrow escapes, I certainly had had one. Perfect as Emily seemed with her artificial red curls, odd fashion sense, and genial disposition, it was simply impossible for me to consider a romantic relationship with someone who wanted to be a college professor.

"So, what?" Travis asked after I had explained

all of this to him. He was fresh out of a surf session, the top of his wetsuit hanging from his torso. Turkey's tail wagged as he snored next to us, his paws resting on Travis's bag.

"I'm throwing in the towel in regard to Emily," I said.

"Yeah, I know, I told you to step off."

"I mean of my own volition." I combed my fingers through the sand. "Like I said, love cannot blossom in the breast of Cecil Haverford when a college professor is involved."

"What's wrong with a college professor? Sounds cool to me. She'd be all smart and stuff. Maybe she'd teach me more about early modern art."

"I didn't think you cared about art. Do you even know what early modern art is?"

"Yeah man, Emily told me. Like, colored squares and stuff with lines going around. Art is awesome."

"I'm surprised, Travis. The last time you mentioned art in my presence was when you got a Hodad's milkshake and said, and I quote 'bro, this is art.'"

Travis made a disdainful noise that sounded like air escaping from a tire. "Whatever, dude," he said, then made the noise again. "Man, that was a good milkshake," he said after a moment of thought.

I shook my head sadly. Poor Travis didn't know what he was getting himself into with this one, and I informed him of this fact. "College professors are notoriously tough old birds. Still, I have to admire your willingness to charge headlong into danger. But anyone facing such peril is going to need some help, and I would be quite an unkind friend if I left you out to hang. Therefore, I am going to help you."

"Dude, I don't need help. I know exactly how to play these things. You wait, like, a week to get her wondering if you're interested, and then when you do call she's all happy and junk."

I shook my head sadly. "No, Travis, I'm afraid that won't work with Emily. You must remember that I have made a thorough study of her character, and I can tell you that this sort of waiting around tomfoolery will not win her heart."

"I don't see what a dude named Tom Fool has to do with anything."

"Listen, you need to call her immediately and invite her on another date. Perhaps a picnic at Balboa Park. Invite Turkey if you wish. He is friendly and will work to your advantage, as long as she doesn't mind a bit of drool, and I think she doesn't. In the meantime, I will put in a good word for you. For instance, I can definitely paint you as a hardworking entrepreneur in the animal care field. Working together, we can't fail."

Travis shrugged, pulled his phone from his bag, and located Emily's number. After saying hello, he slipped the question across to her with a passionate, "So, uh, wanna hang out tonight?" Incredibly spicy stuff. After that he seemed to fizzle out, however, as his part in the conversation consisted mostly of grunts and an, "Oh, okay," at the very end.

"What's the word, then?" I asked. "That didn't sound incredibly promising."

Travis shrugged again. "She said she's busy tonight. She told me she has another date."

I attempted to reel in surprise, but, as you well may have learned at some point yourself, it is nearly impossible to reel in surprise while sitting in the sand.

"What do you mean she has another date?"

"Usually it means she's going out with another dude, bro. She's, like, all about finding a serious relationship, but she thinks she needs to go on tons of dates to find the right guy."

"And I suppose from your tone you find your view on the matter and hers don't entirely coincide."

Travis looked slightly uncomfortable. "I guess not. I kind of think you should only date one person at a time. It just seems weird to be going out with a bunch of people. Like, I don't need to be the Plaid Piper of babes."

I let his mistaken reference to the Pied Piper go so I could focus on the real meat of what he had said. "Is this the absolute truth?" I asked. "I always thought you were one of those loose and casual folks, sweeping though the opposite sex like a wildfire and stepping over the prostrate forms of the broken-hearted. No offense intended, naturally."

Travis became even more uncomfortable and I will swear that he even blushed. "No, bro, I'm not like that. I mean, yeah, I did that a little, but only one at a time, and it never felt right, you know? I think, um, I mean I heard about this thing from someone, where you date someone but don't have sex. It's called Christian Dating. I think I wanna try it."

I know I said how difficult it is to reel in surprise while sitting in the sand, but now I pulled off the feat with all the grace and aplomb of an Olympian at the top of their game. I could think of only one thing to say, and so I said it. "But Travis, what about Bro Code?"

"What do you mean?"

"Well, doesn't converting to Christianity

conflict in some way with it?"

"No, bro, I'm not converting to anything. I'm not into religion. Also, why would Bro Code conflict with Jesus? He was, like, the original bro, doing his posse solids all the time. I just thought that maybe it would be cool to try dating someone without the pressure of all the sex stuff, you know? Like you could just relax and get to know the person. Maybe I would even wait until we got married first, I don't know!"

"In that case I'm confused as to why Christianity enters into the matter at all. Couldn't it be called something non-denominational, like perhaps Abstinence Dating?"

"Dude, I don't get it either, that's just what it's called."

I made a thoughtful noise. Though his delivery could use some work, the substance of Travis's message was clear: he wanted Emily to have eyes only for him, which suited me fine. I try to be modest, but it is a well-known fact that I am a love magnet. In this case, I didn't want to be.

"Don't worry, old chum," I said. "I told you I would support your courtship of Emily, whatever it is you want to call it, and I intend to stick to that."

"No, bro, don't—"

I raised a gentle and understanding hand. "Now, now, I realize you have just bared your soul and are feeling a bit sensitive. By the time you recover I will have come up with a scheme which will be sure to bring the desired results."

Travis made some more sounds of protest, but I was already moving, waving a cheery goodbye to him and Turkey. I returned home to give the matter the thought it deserved. It seemed to me that the course to take would be to call Emily and tell her how Travis felt. It wasn't the sort of thing he should try himself, I decided. They both needed a third party to step in and set the record straight. Once she knew about his aching heart and his soul which bled, she would raise her hand to her fevered brow, say, "Whatever have I done," and rush to his side. Though perhaps bleeding souls was a bit too graphic of imagery. Stick to the aching heart, I told myself as I dialed her number.

"Hello, Cecil?" she said.

"Hello Emily, how are you?"

"Oh, I'm doing okay. It's been a busy day. I had an early morning class. What kind of person schedules a class at 9:30? When I'm a professor I'm not going to have any classes before 11:00!"

"I wholeheartedly agree. It seems the height of irresponsibility. No one can absorb any information that early."

Emily laughed and I had to hold the phone at arm's length for a moment. "Anyway, what's up?" she said.

"Well, as a matter of fact, I did have something particular I wanted to say to you."

"What? Don't say things like that! Now I'm all nervous. You should just say whatever it is and not try to do some sort of preamble. Ugh, hurry up!"

I intended to hurry up, but I found at this point that my mind had gone blank. Thinking back on it, I blame her reaction. Once she got nervous about what I was going to say, so did I. The importance of what I wanted to talk about suddenly hit me. I mean, it's one thing to tell a friend you are going to champion his cause and bring two hearts together as one, but it's quite another to stare the deed in the face and do it. Nevertheless, I had made a promise to Travis, so I steeled my nerves and jumped into it as best I could.

"Do you know about hearts?" I said.

"You mean, like how they work?"

"In a manner of speaking. I mean how a heart will throb."

"That sounds like something a doctor should check out. Do you need to see a doctor, Cecil? I wish I could see a doctor, but I don't have health insurance right now. I mean I guess there's the campus health center, but it doesn't seem like the same thing, you know?"

I briefly wondered how I could have ever been so enamored with Emily. Right when I needed her to stick to the point, she was flitting off to other topics just like a butterfly would if it could converse. "No, I mean how one person's heart throbs for another."

"Cecil, are you talking about love? Do you have a crush on someone?"

"No, no, not me," I said with all the haste I could muster. "I'm speaking for a friend. To you. My friend wanted me to tell you things. About love."

"To me?" She sounded excited. "What did he want you to say?"

"Well, you know, things about hearts throbbing and souls bleeding."

"Souls doing what?"

I felt a warmth on my face, along with a feeling that this was going worse than I had feared. "No, scratch that, the souls aren't doing anything. Ignore the souls."

"Cecil, maybe I should just talk to him myself. Who is it? Is it—" she hesitated. "Is it James?" she finally got out.

"James?" I was incredulous. "No, of course

not. James is dating Violet now."

"Oh, I see." There was an awkward pause. "Well who is he?"

I felt the perspiration beginning to bead. The sensible thing to do would be to tell her it was Travis and wish them both a long and happy life together, but I just couldn't get the words out. Instead I improvised. "He, um, I was, uh, I was sworn to secrecy." I stammered instead. "He is a secret admirer at this point."

There was another awkward pause, this one rather lengthy. "Cecil, you're sweet," Emily said finally. "I've been dating a lot of people lately and I've been having kind of a tough time with both school and work, so I don't think I can deal with having a secret admirer right now. If he wants to talk to me himself then I would listen, but I still can't promise anything because there is a guy I kind of like."

"What?" I cried. "Who is he?"

"Oh no," Emily said with a firecracker giggle. "If you're keeping a secret, then so will I. I have to let you go now."

That seemed to settle that, though it was hardly ideal. I was shaking as I said goodbye to her. Emily not wanting to talk about other suitors because she had someone she was already interested in meant one thing to me: I was in for it. Even I wasn't dense enough to miss the clues. I took a few calming breaths and tried to think clearly about the situation.

Said situation, from what I could tell, looking it over from every angle, seemed, in a word, pretty bad. I had done all I could to plead Travis's case to Emily, and the results were not nearly what I had hoped. It seemed unmistakable that instead of seeing Travis as her one and only, Emily meant to stick with me. I mean to say, if Emily's plan was to scrutinize everyone she had been dating recently and compare their relative pros and cons, I was sure to rise to the top of the pile, and then I would be in for a lifetime with yet another college professor. Where Uncle Gerald ended, Emily would pick up and continue, like a determined relay runner. The only solution that occurred to me was to somehow make myself seem less appealing to her, if that were possible. I decided I would have to think on that some more.

I turned my thoughts instead to Violet and, by extension, James. This was another source of apprehension. Violet expressed what I thought was a disconcerting interest in me because of that *7 Habits of Highly Successful People* book, and I knew I would have to set her straight about that somehow. Frankly, she would be nearly as bad as a college professor. I thought I would need to find some way to improve James's confidence. Given his natural disposition, he was sure to be feeling a little low after getting what amounted to a cold shoulder from Violet the previous night. I had considered them a sure thing, but I realized my mistake was disregarding Violet's sometimes contrary nature. Push a man at her and she would respond with nothing but disdain. The correct approach to use, I realized, would be one of reverse psychology. I would have to point out to her all of James's faults, and then she would react like a mother lion protecting her young, heaping praise on him to counter me, and hopefully believing it. On the other hand, the whole plan could backfire too, since Violet was uncommonly intelligent and might see through my ploy.

My head was feeling rather muddled at this

point. I decided to see if James would want to grab something to eat, and maybe I could work on giving his confidence a shot in the arm. He was at his office, which made things difficult since I didn't know where that was, but I could always call him as I drove there. I grabbed my keys, shod my feet, and went to the door, feeling a funny sense of worry. I remembered the previous time when I had done all those actions and Travis was on the other side of the door, primed and ready to yell at me. I shrugged it off, thinking there was no reason that would happen again. I opened the door and there was Uncle Gerald.

CHAPTER 6

To say I was surprised to see Uncle Gerald would be a gross understatement. A writer of a thesaurus might have done my feelings justice, perhaps by saying I was astounded, amazed, flabbergasted, stupefied, taken aback, or knocked for six. Choose whichever suits you.

What wasn't surprising was Uncle Gerald's displeasure with my terrible showing at the law firm of Tompkins, Richards, and Armstrong. What was surprising was the detailed questions that followed, including how I couldn't remember the law firm's name.

"You don't even know the name?" he shouted at me. "Tompkins, Richards, and Armstrong! That's the name!"

"Well, I've never been good with names, and that's three of them," I tried to explain. "It just popped out of my head."

"I suppose you've also forgotten who it was you were interviewing with."

"Well, yes," I admitted.

"His name, for your information," he said, enunciating every word very particularly for some reason, "is Robert Updike. Does that ring a bell? He is the person who holds your fate in his hands. Remember it!" He sighed and used one hand to rumple his hair before continuing at a more measured volume. "Fortunately, you still have a chance to remedy the situation."

"Is it really that fortunate?" I asked. "Perhaps it's better to just give the whole idea a miss at this point."

Uncle Gerald ignored me. "This is a letter of apology. You are to sign it. You are to put it in this envelope. There is already a stamp on it. You are to then put the envelope in a mailbox. This is a map to the nearest one. I have gone out of my way to make this foolproof. I don't know how you could possibly mess this up, but I would not be surprised if you find a way."

"I shall not disappoint," I said. "I mean, I shall not disappoint in completing the task, not that I will not disappoint in fulfilling your expectation of my failure. What I mean is there is no reason to worry."

Uncle Gerald glared at me like a serpent ready to strike. "See that there isn't," he said.

"By the way, what on earth are you doing here?"

"I told you I had a conference here," he stated simply.

"Ah, yes, the mists of memory begin to clear, and it all comes back to me. Did you perhaps mention how long this conference would last?"

Uncle Gerald flashed me a tight, wicked smile,

and then he was gone. He must have marched or strode from the room as any normal person would, but my impression was that he silently evaporated, like breath off cold glass.

I sagged under the crushing weight of an uncle's disappointment until I settled on the couch. This was just the cap to the day's events that I needed. Then I realized it wasn't half past one yet and there was undoubtedly more to come. "Death, where be thy sting?" I moaned.

Fortunately, we Haverfords are made of tough stuff. Though we might be down, we are never out. It wasn't the best and brightest Cecil Haverford who ever rose from that couch, but rise he, by which I mean I, did, determined to soldier on. After all, I just needed to send a letter. More importantly, it gave me an idea for how to help James with his confidence.

"James, I have an idea for how to help you," I said once James returned home. I, myself, had had a hot bath and an afternoon nap, being much too overcome to venture anywhere outdoors. But, with those taken care of and James in my presence, I was ready for action.

"What do I need help with?" James asked. He was again dressed in a surprisingly dapper manner for a weekday evening.

"Do you normally dress like that? I know you had a suit on for the interview, and naturally you would try for a date, but there is no special occasion now."

"Oh, I guess so. I mean I like to dress well, you know?"

I nodded. "I hadn't noticed before, but this is good. You may have noticed that Violet also tends to be impeccable in her appearance. Quite a match you two will make."

"Yeah about that." James scratched his head. "I just don't know if there's much of a connection there. I didn't feel a spark. Frankly, she seemed to ignore me."

I tutted. "Nonsense, you two are absolutely high voltage. You just need to step up your game, as it were. Have some emotional appeal, some vulnerability."

James fidgeted. "I guess so. I can be a little reserved sometimes. But I think that maybe a girl should just like me for the way I am. If I act differently I might not find someone suited to me."

I nodded. "Certainly you should be yourself, but a girl has to have an opportunity to get to know you, right? That involves being bold and taking a chance!" I slapped him on the back. "Fortunately, I have the perfect solution, crafted specifically for your disposition. You should write a letter to her."

I expected this to go over big, but it fizzled. Instead of jumping up and down while smacking his forehead in amazement, James just made a face. "Isn't that kind of old fashioned?" he asked.

"Nonsense, it will be seen as romantic and soulful," I said, trying to salvage the idea. "And it is perfectly well suited to the psychology of both of you. What you can't say in words, you will write. What she may not have the time in her schedule to listen to, she will read while doing something else like exercising or watering plants or reading something else. You can imagine, I'm sure."

"No one can read two things at once," James said.

"You're just being pedantic now. Don't

underestimate Violet's powers of multitasking. I'm telling you this will be just the thing."

"I guess it could be a good idea, but I'm not sure I could really write a letter like that."

"I have already thought of that, my dear friend. I will write the letter for you. This way you can't help but succeed." I struck what I hoped was a sophisticated, trustworthy pose. "You will recall, I'm sure, that I am a professional freelance writer."

"Yep, I know that," James said in a way that indicated a displeasure with my flair for the dramatic.

"Ah, good. So then you can rest assured that I will deliver on my promise."

"Do I get any say as to what goes into this letter?"

I gave a genial chuckle. "You need not worry about the content. I will take care of all the little details. Just trust me."

He shrugged, looking a bit exasperated. "I don't know what to say. Maybe this will work. Maybe I even want it to work. I'm not sure. This is just so sudden." He eyed me. "Are you sure this girl Violet actually likes me?"

I nodded. "I understand. There's a saying about this attitude you have, something about letting 'I dare not' wait upon 'I would.' Like a cat, or a possum, maybe. I say seize the day! Let the world be your oyster. Grasp that oyster by the shell and gulp it with gusto. The oyster, not the shell."

James buried his head in his hands. "Cecil, I just don't know," he said, somewhat muffled. "I brought some work home with me I need to finish up now. Please don't do anything crazy. Let me think about this."

I patted him on the shoulder, said a few pleasant nothings to make him feel better, and watched as he ambled over to his room. He hadn't exactly said yes, but then he hadn't exactly said no, either. Anyway, he had said to not do anything crazy, and I didn't think anything in this scheme would be considered crazy. Once Violet received the letter, she would be whipped into such a romantic frenzy towards James that when I insulted him to her, as I still planned on doing, no doubt she would come through with the desired result. It was as perfect and sensible as clockwork.

I set to drafting the letter. As I worked, it occurred to me that the idea which would help James and Violet find love would also help Travis and Emily. True, I had already attempted something like this over the phone, but that was where I had made my mistake. As I mentioned previously, I am simply no good over the phone. But give me pen and paper, or more realistically keyboard and computer, and I am solid gold. Once Emily had read the letter I wrote from Travis, I would come around to talk myself down and talk him up, and then everything would be, as they say, hunky dory. I made sure to make the wording vague enough to apply to either woman, as I felt that the sentiment was very much the same for both of them, and therefore it would be silly to write two letters. I eventually ended up with the following:

Dear (insert name),

I am writing to inform you of a passion burning in my breast. This passion, which by the way is for you, began when I first laid eyes upon you. It was as though Prometheus arrived with the secret of fire and lit my heart ablaze. I can only lay my blazing, smoldering heart, a heart which smolders for you, before your feet and hope against hope that you will return my feelings.

Please, when you receive this, call Cecil Haverford and let him know of your feelings. If they were unfavorable, I could not bear to hear them from you with mine own ears.

Yours faithfully,
An Admirer

As I said, solid gold. I felt that if this didn't bring two individuals together and unite them as one in love forever, I had no idea what would. Undoubtedly Violet, or Emily, as the case may be, would see the letter and call me, as instructed. Then I would proceed with my part of it, and before you could say "marriage," Cupid's arrows would have done their thing and everything would be all a wonderful story that is told to the grandchildren.

I needed addresses to send these to, so I crafted a subtle inquiry to send via text message. It read "Hello, could I perhaps have your address? Not for any real reason at all." This was fantastic in getting results, at least from Emily. Violet was a bit more distrustful, but fortunately I had seen that coming. When she asked why I needed it, I said I thought I would get her something for her birthday, which was several weeks away. She accepted this explanation with some reserve, and I got the result I was after.

I whistled happily as I stuffed the envelopes, even taking the initiative to include Uncle Gerald's apology letter in the mix, which would no doubt have impressed everyone who knew me. After addressing and applying stamps to the envelopes, I ran them downstairs, followed Uncle Gerald's map to a blue postal drop box, and shoved them in. The door of the box closed with a very satisfying clang, a clang of cheerful finality.

The job finished, I decided to stop in at a local

alehouse for some food and drink. Satisfied in mind, body, and spirit, I returned home and threw a cheery hello to James, who had come out from hiding.

"You seem like you're in a good mood," he said.

"Yes, I am now," I said. "I didn't tell you at the time, but I had an odious letter to send for my Uncle Gerald. Thankfully I sent that along with the one I wrote for you."

"You didn't!" James cried. "Cecil, I asked you not to!"

"You actually didn't," I pointed out.

"Well I certainly said I wasn't comfortable with it. I can't believe you did that!"

"It's not like you're the only one, you know. I sent one for Travis, too. You remember Travis, right? He's dating Emily."

"I thought you were dating Emily." James clutched his head with one hand. "This is so confusing. Tell me from the beginning."

I filled him in on the goings on, how love with Emily was dead, about the two copies of the letter I sent out, and even a brief word on Travis's Christian Dating scheme.

"This isn't happening," James said hollowly. "I mean, how could you think it was a good idea to send the same letter to two people?"

"Well it seemed unnecessary to actually write two letters. No need to do the same thing twice, right? It would just be a waste of time."

"Cecil, you have a very unique, distinctive writing style, don't you?" James asked patiently.

I nodded. "I do. I pride myself on it, in fact."

"So don't you suppose that they will figure out who actually wrote the letters? And then what will they think? This is forgery, you know. I mean, not actually. It's definitely questionable behavior."

I rubbed a meditative chin. "Let me see if I understand what you're saying. You think that, because of the writing style, Violet and Emily will know that I was the originator of the letters. Furthermore, you think they will inevitably collude, if collude is the word, to discuss the matter and discover that both letters are identical. This discovery will lead them to think that at best I am making fun of them and at worst I am a creeping scoundrel plotting some sort of evil, malevolent scheme with no clear payoff other than mayhem and destruction. Is that what you're saying?"

"I'm saying you're going to have two women pissed at you, but sure, let's go with that."

"I'm not convinced that will happen. I will just feign ignorance, and any inquiries on the matter will be met with said ignorance. Letters? I don't know anything about these letters of which you speak."

"Okay, but you told me that you asked them for their addresses. Won't that be at all suspicious to them?"

"I will just say I was asking for you and Travis. You see, this plan is absolutely flawless."

"That's debatable. For instance, what did you put for the return address? You didn't just write down your name and address, did you?"

I started rubbing my neck and cast my mind back. I couldn't say that I hadn't done that, when I really thought about it. A sort of tingling feeling started up my spine, and as it reached the top it blossomed into a warm buzzing across my scalp and forehead.

James was going on. "And going back to the matter of the women getting together to compare notes, that would be really bad. The same exact note word for word? You couldn't say you coached us both to write the same exact thing to them."

The warm buzzing was turning into a very feverish feeling, and it was starting to make me panicky. "I thought that, well, you know, I thought… hum," I finished on a weak note as my mind worked. While James could be correct in supposing Violet and Emily to be angry at me over the letters, another, more sinister possibility arose in my mind. Seeing those letters and deducing that they were written by me, they might find their attitudes towards me softened even more.

All the implications of my actions washed over me like ocean water over a freshly stubbed toe. I patted my pockets, hoping that somehow I had forgotten to put the letters into the drop box, but that was not the case. I remembered the clang of the door which shortly before seemed so delightful to me. Now sounded like a death knell. "James, do you know how to break into a postal drop box?"

CHAPTER 7

Perhaps you have not experienced this in your personal life, so let me tell you that once the machinery of the postal service begins, it is absolutely impossible to halt. I tried like mad to alter the course of those letters, cajoling, begging, and even once resorting to threatening the postal employees. Someday I will write a book of life advice, and in that book I will be sure to advise that no one ever, under any circumstances, threaten a postal employee; they are tough as nails.

All this is to say that two days later I was still on pins and needles about those letters. Fortunately, I hadn't put all my chickens in the bush, or however the saying goes. I had also been devising contingencies. My last hope, I felt, was to grab the letters myself as they were delivered, which promised to be an adventure fraught with peril. Snatching them from the mailbox before Emily or Violet could get them would be an easy solution, but it was one that filled me with dread. I had no desire to be caught by some nosy neighbor while digging through someone else's mailbox. The other option was to gain access to their homes and snag the letters before they were opened. It was dicey, but I thought it would be the best option available to me.

That left me deciding whose letter I should abscond with first, Violet or Emily. I was torn on this. As I considered the pros and cons of each case, I found my mind working itself into increasingly complex knots. I needed organization. James had often told me about the virtues of spreadsheets, so I figured I would give one a try.

I drafted the spreadsheet to track what I thought the risks were, both for if they read the letters and if I were discovered trying to take the letters. Then I assigned numerical values to each entry based on how awful I thought they were and tallied the whole thing up. I started at the number it gave me for a moment but could glean no insight from it.

"James, you're wrong," I said as I left my room. "Spreadsheets are of no use to anyone."

"You have to make them right," James said patiently. "I tell you this every time. Why are you making a spreadsheet?"

"I'm trying to decide who I should burgle my letter from first. Who do you think?"

James gave his head an emphatic shake. "No, leave me out of this. You made this bed, now you can lie in it."

"Fine, then I shall ask Travis." I about faced back into my room to call him.

"Who what now?" Travis asked after I explained my predicament, omitting names so he wouldn't get angry. I hadn't told him about sending a letter to Emily, after all.

"You heard me," I said. "How would you decide who to take the letter from first."

"I dunno, flip a coin."

I shrugged and did so. It came up tails, so Emily it was.

Emily lived out by her university, somewhat to the east of what many people consider San Diego proper, in a place called La Mesa. I am told this translates to "The Mesa," but don't take my word for it. Being inland as it is, the temperature is noticeably warmer. When it might be a pleasant 75 degrees Fahrenheit where I resided, out in La Mesa it could easily be up to 90. A little rough on the body for my tastes, but some people seem to actually take pleasure in it. Plants certainly didn't seem to enjoy it, unless they were actually local to the area. Most of these were some form of totally brown bush or tree. The environment is simply lacking the necessary water for delightful and abundant green plant life.

The neighborhood Emily lived in was characterized by twisting, labyrinthine roads which appeared to rearrange themselves at whim. After circling the same half-dozen streets for 20 minutes, I finally found Emily's address and cast an appraising eye over the house which squatted there. One story, equipped with a garage, and presumably there was a back yard with landscaping designed to be easily maintained, such as concrete, or gravel, since it was probably rented to students most often. I was correct, as it turns out, and it was in fact a rental house which she shared with several other people.

I wasn't entirely sure on my approach, so I parked my car a good distance from the house in case stealth was required. Though it was against my better judgment, I couldn't help but peek in the mailbox, just in case that would solve everything, but it was empty. I walked up to the front door, wondering what I would do now. I looked around a bit for alternatives, but I saw none, so I steeled myself and knocked.

There was no answer for some time, and I was beginning to worry that I wouldn't be able to get in without actions of questionable legality. I knocked again louder, and this time I heard a rustling within. The door opened and a thin male specimen with greasy hair down to his shoulders and a wispy goatee gave me a sullen look.

"'Sup?" he said.

I quickly attached an ingratiating smile to my face. "Hello, is Emily in?" I asked.

"Nah," he said. "She's out."

This seemed to simplify matters. I could just slip in, find where the mail was, and grab my letter. The only problem was this fellow wasn't giving me much to work with. A simple "Would you like to come in?" would have been ideal at this moment, but it was plainly not forthcoming. I resolved to take matters into my own hands, and immediately sprang into action. "Would it be all right if I came in for a bit and waited for her?" I asked.

The specimen shrugged and shuffled a few feet away from the door. I took this as a sign that I was welcome, so I entered, looked around, and gave a small shudder at what I saw. The interior décor, if it could be called that, was awful. Furniture seemed to be scattered with no rhyme nor reason. Chairs were facing in random directions, a sofa squatted in front of the fireplace, and end tables lurked in the places where you would most likely trip on them. I had been living with

James's masterful aesthetic sense for some time, so it was overwhelming to take in. The Cecil Haverford of last year might not have batted an eye upon entering this room, but the Cecil Haverford who had been educated in flow, balance, and keeping a walkway clear was shaken to the depths of his soul.

After taking a moment to adjust my eyes to the chaos, I spied a table overflowing with envelopes. No doubt that was where they kept the mail, though how I would find my letter in that mess was something I couldn't figure out at the moment. I was expecting to pluck it out of a mail sorter or, at worse, the top of a mostly clear table. I didn't think I would have to organize a search party. "When do you expect Emily to return?" I asked, trying to figure out how much time I had.

The specimen shrugged again, clearly deciding he was done with me and didn't need to waste any more air. He then turned and disappeared down a hallway.

I heaved a sigh, glad to have him out of my life, and turned to the pile of mail. I didn't have the foggiest idea how to begin. I had visions of me being like that one fellow who always had to push a stone up a hill, only in this case I would be sorting mail in a dreadfully decorated house, and it was hard to say who had it worse. I wouldn't be doing it eternally as he was forced to, since presumably Emily would be home sometime before forever occurred, but that in a way made it worse. Imagine if you had to push a stone up a hill while at any moment a budding young college professor could show up and tell you fifteen ways you are doing it wrong. It was that sort of pressure I was working under.

I had just sat down to start when I heard voices

outside. I froze, listening closely to hear who it was. My worst fear was that Emily was returning, but that, I suddenly realized, would not be so bad. I had been invited in, probably, and I realized, in a flash of inspiration, I could say I was there to talk to her about Travis.

Life has a way of making what you imagine to be your worst fears seem tiny and insignificant. So, while I wasn't too concerned to hear Emily's voice on the other side of the door, a sudden chill shot through my stomach when I heard Violet's. My heart immediately started trying to leap out of my throat and the room took on a hazy, rippling appearance, as if it was a mirage seen from far away in the desert.

I felt like I had been standing there for several hours, though it must have been only a few seconds. Then I heard the rattle and scrape of a key in the door's lock, and I immediately leapt into action. I didn't at first know where I was leaping, so it came as some surprise to me when I found myself both behind a sofa and crammed partway into a fireplace. It was an uncomfortable and disorienting position to be in, and it would be even more uncomfortable if I was found. I told myself that it was a very good hiding spot, well hidden from the casual observer, but I was still anxious.

"What was that noise?" Violet asked as the two of them entered the room.

"Probably Mark, my roommate," Emily said. "I don't really know what he's up to when he's home. Usually he stays in his room, doing something or other. I don't think I've heard a noise from him in a couple of months."

Violet murmured an indistinct reply. I assumed she

was taking in the room, a task which doesn't allow a person to have well thought out responses. "This place is… nice," she said. I knew that Violet was dissembling, dissembling being a word which means "to lie through her teeth." She has always had a distinct sense of style when it comes to her personal dwelling, almost approaching James's. I remember when she went so far as to cram a Chesterfield sofa into her dorm room during her freshman year at college. I have no idea where she slept, but her side of the room was set up well enough to comfortably host a party of six. For her to compliment a place like this must have meant that she either really liked Emily and genuinely wanted to be nice, or she really disliked Emily and wanted to seem superior and gracious. I've seen it go either way with her.

"Anyway, I really think you'll like this show," Emily said. "It's got some action, but not too much, and it's romantic and funny. It's just great!"

"What it sounds like to me," Violet said, "is that it's a show which pushes female empowerment through makeup and jewelry."

"It doesn't! Not too much anyway. I mean, that's not really the main point. It's more about discovering yourself and what you're good at, I think. And it's about fighting monsters and saving the ones you love."

"Through the power of makeup and jewelry." Violet repeated wryly.

Emily made a frustrated noise. "Just watch one! You'll like it, you really will." It sounded like she was dragging Violet down the hallway. I inferred from the noise of a door closing that I was safe for the moment and emerged from hiding.

I didn't know what show they were going to watch

or how long it was. In the worst case I had about twenty minutes to search for my letter. Or less, I corrected myself, since Violet could get fed up with it and refuse to watch more.

What the greater part of me wanted at that moment was to sneak out and never return, but that would lead to dire consequences. If Emily found that letter, especially with Violet here to read it also, I would be in for it. I heaved a heavy sigh and again approached the pile of mail.

There is a certain psychological effect which occurs when a person looks at a stack of unopened mail. It gives one a panicked, nervous feeling in the chest, along with an urge to run to the nearest TV and perch in front of it for the next several hours. I was feeling that sensation as I began sorting through the envelopes, but as I continued a curious thing began to occur. I felt an overwhelming sense of relief at the fact that I didn't have to deal with any of these things. None of them were for me. Not the month-old bills which may or may not have been paid yet, not any of the annoying coupons, not the letters from half-forgotten friends who, in a fit of hipster enthusiasm, decided to use traditional mail. It was astonishingly freeing, and I strongly encourage anyone who is having a rough day to just look through another person's mail and feel what I felt.

That aside, there was a lot of mail and it took quite a number of minutes to find what I was seeking, but find it I did. I had been so focused on the emotional journey I was taking, I completely forgot about the time. I was startled when I heard a door open followed by voices in the hallway. There was another round of stomach chilling, heart-leaping, and wavering vision, after which I again made the dash for the backside of the couch. To be completely honest though, it was all becoming a bit routine at this point, lacking perhaps the *joie de vivre* it once had, if that is the term I want. What I mean is I was getting a bit sick of it and I wanted out, now that I had the letter.

"I did think it was a little bit funny," Violet was saying. "But what was with that tuxedo guy?"

Emily laughed. "Wasn't it great when he said crying wouldn't solve anything, but then it totally solved everything?"

"Yes, I appreciated the irony, but was he really there just to berate her?"

"No, he mostly shows up to throw a rose and then do nothing."

"What a man," Violet said, presumably mock swooning, though I couldn't see it from my position.

It's always difficult when two people are talking about a piece of media that a third person, perhaps someone stuck in a cramped hiding place nearby, is not familiar with. I stopped paying attention and let my mind wander for a bit, but I was called back quickly by something Emily said.

"Oh, what's this envelope?"

The stomach chilling, heart-leaping, and wavering vision suddenly had all the zest and joy they initially had. I tried to pat myself to see if perhaps this was a different envelope and if the one I wanted was on my person, but the action was just impossible.

"It has Haverford's return address," Violet sniffed. "I wonder why he's writing you."

There was a stage wait while the envelope was opened and the contents read. Then came the cracking report of Emily's laughter. "Why is he apologizing so formally?" she gasped. Once she contained herself she continued. "I knew him calling me like that was just some sort of joke. Oh, that's such a relief. I was worried he would confront me in some way, and then I would have to hope for some sweet, gentle soul with puppy-dog eyes to rescue me."

Violet made a disdainful noise, sort of a mix between a growl and a snort. "You could just tell him off yourself. That's what I'm going to do. He seems completely unbalanced. I don't know what he's thinking right now."

"I don't know if that's necessary. He seems like he really regrets it."

I probably don't need to tell you how surprising this all was to me. I was completely at a loss. I believed I had sent love letters to both of these women, but one of them received an apology letter. I couldn't make heads nor tails of it for a moment, and then with a start, or as much of one as I could make in my confined situation, I realized what must have happened. The apology letter Uncle Gerald wanted me to send must have gotten into the envelope meant for Emily, and the apology therein must have been vague enough to make Emily think it was intended for her. Probably it began with, "To whom it may concern," which I know from personal experience is a favorite opener of Uncle Gerald's. I reached the conclusion that this meant the letter intended for Emily was at this very moment making its way towards Robert Updike. The thought sent a shiver through me.

Fortune chose that moment to go easy on me. "I should be going now," Violet said. "Thanks for the show. It was interesting and amusing. I'll ask Haverford about these letters the next time I see him."

"Are you close friends?" Emily asked.

"It's complicated. I don't really have time to get into it, and I don't want to have our conversations monopolized by Haverford anyway."

"I suppose you can have your secrets and I'll respect that. Like I won't ask why you call him by his last name all the time, even though it's such a weird thing to do."

Violet laughed a little. "Don't worry about that, it's just a habit." The two women said their goodbyes and then they left, one stage left, the other stage right. That was how it sounded to me, anyway.

I waited for a moment, hoping I wouldn't run into either of the two while I was leaving. In particular I wanted to avoid Violet, who, unless I was very much mistaken, had left via the front door. When I judged that the time was right, I crept out from behind the couch and saw the greasy-haired specimen who had initially opened the door, presumably Mark the roommate, staring at me. I dusted myself off in what I hoped was an elegant and refined manner, then said to him "I'll be leaving now. You needn't tell Emily I was here. Thank you for your hospitality."

My morale was low as I left, by which I mean I was bummed out, to use a phrase I have heard Travis employ frequently. I had failed utterly and miserably, and it seemed as if the world held no joy. The skies hadn't actually darkened, this being Southern California, where the skies never truly darken for anything, but they seemed darker to me. The plants looked wilted and lifeless, and while there was nothing new there, it didn't help my mood. It will tell you the state of my mind when I say that without so much as a glance or a kind hello I passed what I assumed to be one of the local residents, a woman with fine, lifeless straw-colored hair, wearing dark jeans and a frumpy polo shirt, who was struggling with the door to her car. I would have continued in my daze if a voice hadn't arrested me at that moment.

"Haverford? What are you doing here?" The voice sounded brittle, cold, and surprisingly like Violet's. I turned around and saw the woman I had just passed approaching me.

"What? I—I," I stammered, not entirely grasping what was occurring, but getting a sense that the person in front of me was, in fact, Violet.

"What are you doing here? Are you trying to bother Emily?" I wanted to say that I would like nothing more than to never bother Emily again, but she swept on before I could even begin to speak. "Never mind, I have something I want to ask you about."

That was too much for me. I was alarmed at having run into Violet, and completely confused by her appearance. It was so unlike what I was used to seeing from her that I was dumbstruck. To have her say she needed to ask me something on top of that put me over. The world reeled around me and I felt faint. I began to topple forward and caught myself on something. When I regained my senses a moment later, I found myself in an awkward embrace with Violet.

"I'm going to give you to the count of three to let go of me," she said.

CHAPTER 8

Once I had recovered myself a bit I peered at Violet. She had none of the trappings which were her signature. No fine coiffure perched on her head. No form fitting dressings of any kind. There also seemed to be something odd about her face which took me a moment to place.

"Violet, you're wearing glasses!" I cried.

Violet gave me one of her best glares, the sort which pierces through any sort of eyewear straight to the soul and chills the bones down to the marrow. At least that part of her hadn't changed. "I came here straight from work," she growled.

"What sort of job are you doing dressed like that?" I wondered aloud.

"I'm a computer scientist! How do you not know that?"

I shrugged. "But still—" I began.

"No, I won't hear it," she said. "This is what a computer scientist wears to work. I often enjoy dressing like a woman, but not when I'm spending my time around people whose favorite topic of conversation is how awful it is that a programming language we don't even use does not require semicolons after every line!"

I didn't quite understand what she was talking about with semicolons, but I did acknowledge the legitimacy of the point she raised. I also saw that she was in absolutely top form today, and if I wasn't careful I would get an earful the likes of which I haven't heard since we were in our Junior year together and she yelled for ten minutes straight over my neglecting to visit an academic advisor for one semester. It seemed to me at the time that once you had seen them and gotten a plan, there was no reason for a second visit. Needless to say, Violet had visited an academic advisor regularly, sometimes even going mid-semester to ensure that the machinery of education was still humming along nicely.

"Haverford are you listening to me?" Violet asked.

I looked up with a start. Violet was getting the familiar look she would always get when conversing with me alone for some time. She looked sore as a boil, and I tried my best to change the subject from what we had been talking about.

"Nice weather today, eh?" I said, casting about for inspiration and seeing only the unchanging blue sky which lurks over the greater part of Southern California all year round.

"Don't you try to change the subject or distract me with irrelevancies," Violet said, going so far as to stamp her foot, a gesture I had never seen someone do in real life. "I want to know what the hell those letters are about."

I was stunned into silence for a moment. It

wasn't the mention of the letters that did it; I had heard her say she wanted to question me about them. It was her choice of words that surprised me. As long as I had known her, Violet was one of those people who never uttered a curse word. That she would use a word as strong as "hell" concerned me. I decided to follow up on that.

"Violet, you never used to use such language," I said.

"What, hell? Haverford, I say much worse these days, especially after work."

I was absolutely blown away by this news. She could have told me that she was about to embark on a thirty day diet of water and the ethers in the air and I would have been less surprised. "Since when?" I asked.

"If I tell you, will you answer my question?"

"Which question was that?"

"The letters, Haverford!" Violet repeated her foot stamping.

I said something along the lines of "ah" and considered for a moment. "I just don't know if I'm that curious," I finally decided.

Violet looked down her nose at me. Even in a polo shirt and jeans and with her hair uncombed, she had the regal bearing which made me feel like dust beneath her feet. "Haverford, you will tell me what you meant by sending those letters."

I sighed. There was no arguing against that tone of voice. Violet meant to pry the information from me with her bare hands if she needed to. "If you must know, I was trying to further the interests of love."

"Love?" Violet snorted. "With that?"

"Yes, absolutely," I sniffed, a little defensively.

"And what about the one to Emily?" Violet looked at me closely as she said that. "That apology? What was that about?"

"That was a mistake," I said. "That letter was supposed to be received by Robert Updike of Tompkins, Richards, and Armstrong."

"Why were you apologizing to him?"

"I vomited on his desk during a job interview."

Violet nodded. "Yes, that sounds like something you would do." She paused and tapped her forefinger against her cheek, a sign that her mind was working furiously. "So, should I presume that there was a letter like mine meant to go to Emily?"

"It's not like they were exactly the same," I said, suddenly ashamed.

"If you say so. Should I also assume that that letter went to Robert Updike?"

"You know how it is," I tried to explain. "You have letters and envelopes. You try to put them in their proper spots, but sometimes they just leap about and go where they shouldn't. There was really no way this could have been avoided."

"I don't think that statement is true, but we'll leave that for now. What I can't figure out is why you need Robert Updike's approval so much. Yes, it was a catastrophic job interview at a place you have no right applying to…" she paused. "Oh, I've got it. It's something about your uncle, isn't it?"

I nodded. "Uncle Gerald says he will cut off the support he and Uncle Ted provide me, so I must procure this job. My having failed once, he personally penned an apology which I was to send. Now Robert Updike will have a letter from my address in which a secret admirer professes love for him."

Violet made a noise which sounded like a choked off laugh. I looked up at her. Her frosty demeanor was beginning to show cracks of amusement. "You may as well laugh," I said forlornly. "I fear I am ruined, with no possible avenue of action available to me."

Her smile broke out fully and she gave a smug toss of her head. "Don't worry, I'll straighten things out with Uncle Bobby."

I was confused. "Uncle who?"

"Robert Updike."

I gasped. "Violet, did my ears deceive me? You're not actually related to that old puff of hot air?"

"He married my aunt on my mother's side. He's a very unpleasant person, but for some reason he adores me. He'll listen to what I say."

"Violet, I don't know how I can repay you," I said. "What an astounding coincidence! Who'd have thought you would be niece to that man? It's mind boggling."

"Don't mention it. You are my friend after all. But really, I'm concerned. I've known you to pull some silly stunts, but nothing on this level. Are you okay?"

"I feel absolutely ebullient," I assured her.

"Yes, but I mean do you—" she hesitated. "Do you need to talk about anything? Like maybe your—"

"No, thank you," I cut her off.

"Haverford, you know I'm just concerned for you."

"I wish you would call me Cecil sometimes."

Violet shook her head firmly. "You know I won't do that. This was our compromise."

I stiffened. "Of course. I wish to thank you for your assistance in the matter of Robert Updike," I said as formally as I could. "If there isn't anything else, I shall be taking my leave now."

Violet sighed, then shrugged. "You should tell Mr. Winters what's going on with Uncle Bobby before he finds out himself. Let him know that things are under control. Take care, Haverford. I'll be in touch."

I nodded numbly, then turned and wound my way back to my car. Once there, I sat with my mind in a jumble. Violet just had to be so nosy about everything, and so good at figuring things out. It was sometimes infuriating, but also sometimes it could be helpful. I thought her suggestion about letting Uncle Gerald know what was going on was a good one.

I pulled out my phone and commenced the call. Once we had dispensed with the hellos, I gave it to him straight, starting with the bad news. "I'm afraid I sent Richard Updike a love letter," I said.

"I think the connection is bad," he said. "I didn't hear what you said clearly."

"Mr. Robert Updike has by now undoubtedly opened a love letter signed by a secret admirer and sent by me. But," I went on quickly before he could say anything, "the situation is well under control."

Uncle Gerald had begun sputtering, but he managed to switch it off. "You sent Robert Updike a love letter and you're telling me it's under control? What the hell happened?"

I winced. "Uncle Gerald, please, your language. I was sending out some other letters at the same time as his, and they got mixed up."

"Ah, so instead of working on securing employment you've been gallivanting about, making love to every person you see, is that it?" His voice was beginning to rise in pitch.

"Not at all. I was taking some time to assist a friend, it's true, but I assure you that this task you've given me has been at the forefront of my mind. I've even enlisted the assistance of Robert Updike's very own niece to set things to rights."

"Not Violet Andrews," Uncle Gerald said, his voice iron.

"I didn't know you knew each other." I began to wonder if there was anyone Violet didn't know.

"She was in a class I taught once," Uncle Gerald said in a tone that caused me to imagine a faraway look in his eye as he remembered. "Never have I had a more difficult class."

"She assured me she will be able to handle everything."

"I hope so," Uncle Gerald said before ending the connection.

My mind whirled as I drove home. It seemed like the most outrageous coincidence that Uncle Gerald and Violet should know each other. I felt the only thing that could possibly top that was if Violet somehow knew someone like Travis, but that was too far-fetched to ever actually happen.

As I turned my key in the lock and opened the door, I heard a peculiar noise, a sort of rustling thump. My recent experiences gave me a very good notion as to exactly what it was I heard, and I made a beeline for the sofa. I found the gap between the back of the sofa and the wall was filled to the brim with the tangled mess of Travis and Turkey. It seemed like a sea of arms, legs, and wagging tails back there. "'Sup dude," Travis said as nonchalantly as he could.

CHAPTER 9

When one finds someone, even a friend and a friend's dog, hidden behind a sofa, naturally one must inquire as to why. It was with the spirit of inquiry that I asked, "Travis, what are you doing here? And I don't mean just in my apartment. Why are you nestled behind my couch in what I can only describe as a sinister way? Not that I can really complain without seeming like the most egregious hypocrite. You wouldn't believe the day I've had."

I'm sure Travis was expecting recrimination, shouting, and generally unpleasant behavior from me. To tell the truth though, I just couldn't bring myself to do it. As I said it would be hypocrisy of the highest order to scold and punish him for something I had done myself not even an hour ago. But the main reason I remained so even keeled was that I was just too exhausted from recent events. I couldn't raise my voice above a murmur, to say nothing of leaping about in an agitated manner, which is what I pictured having to do. And thus, Travis lay there, confused at my lack of anger at his presence behind my sofa.

Travis is never one to be stunned for long. Already I could see in his eyes he was coming to grips with the situation and would be ready to converse in no time.

"So yeah, funny seeing you here," he said as he heaved himself out from behind the couch. Turkey crawled out slowly, wheezing a little as he did.

"I do live here, you know," I said. "It would be expected to eventually run into me if you continue to haunt the areas behind my furniture. Not that I'm upset," I added, seeing him begin to brace himself.

"You're not?" He asked.

"No, I'm not. I am curious what you're doing here though."

"That's easy, bro," Travis said. He paused for a moment, like an orchestra preparing to launch into a tricky piece of music, such as *An American in Paris.* I had a funny feeling as I watched him that he had spent months fine tuning and practicing what he was about to say, even though that couldn't possibly be the case. I perched myself on the edge of the couch, eager to hear the beautiful tapestry which was about to be woven for me.

"So, like, I was just out, you know, doing my thing, and I thought I should stop by and see my best bro. That's you."

I graciously acknowledged the compliment and motioned for him to continue.

"So, I came up and you weren't here, but your roommate was, so I was like hey man can I come in and he was like sure thing dude. So yeah, here I am."

I nodded. "So far, so good, but why did you choose to recline in the space behind the sofa?"

"Oh, well, see, I was just chilling here waiting for you when Turkey got up to some trouble." Travis shot an admonishing glance at Turkey, who was still wheezing a bit.

"What sort of trouble would this be?" I asked.

"Okay, so you know those socks you have?"

"My socks?" I wasn't quite sure where he was trying to go with this.

"Yeah, those ones that you love."

"You mean the orange argyle socks?" I said, inventing a lie.

Travis wrinkled his nose at me. "Really bro? Orange socks? Oh I mean, yeah, those ones. So, like, Turkey found them and started chewing them."

"They were in my sock drawer, Travis," I lied again. I was beginning to enjoy myself.

"Yeah, he opened the drawer," he said, barely missing a beat. "Turkey's not a chump, dude, he's smart. So, like I was saying, he opened the drawer, got the socks out and started chewing them, and I was all like, aw man, no Turkey, that's so not cool, but he was like, whatever I'm just gonna chomp these socks like I don't care." Travis did a remarkable pantomime of Turkey chewing a sock, then looked me straight in the eye. "And he totally didn't care, bro. He didn't care."

"Turkey spoke?"

"No, man, that's dumb. 'Course he didn't. But I could tell what he was thinking from his eyes."

"I see, my mistake. So how did this lead to your placement when I came in?"

Travis nodded his head. "I'm getting there, dude. So like, I grabbed the socks, but Turkey fought back, and I was like oh man, no Turkey, that'll stretch them out! But he just growled and tugged and then he pulled us behind the couch and I fell over. Then you came in."

"Very good, Travis, but there is one small detail you have omitted. Where are the socks now?"

Travis pondered my question for a moment. "Turkey ate them," he said.

I glanced at Turkey. He gave a sort of wheezing hiccup, or maybe a coughing gasp and looked at me innocently. I shook my head. "Travis, I don't have a pair of socks like that," I told him, then I raised a hand to stop his protest. "Now, now, I've caught you red-handed and we both know it. But that's fine."

"No, bro, really, I need to explain," Travis began, but Turkey interrupted him with another hiccup or cough, or maybe it was a moan, and then an awful retching. I watched in disgust as he spat up what looked like a small, moist wad of paper. Travis clutched his head. "Ah, Turkey, no dude, bad dog. You were supposed to keep that down."

"And what is that?" I asked.

"Okay, bro, I'll tell you what really happened. I got all twisted up inside because I was worried you would think I'm weird about the Christian Dating thing. So I was like, okay, I'm gonna write a list of things about Cess that suck and then he won't be able to make fun of me. So I did that, right, and today I came to tell you them. But you weren't here, so I was thinking about it and I decided it was kind of lame anyway. So I fed the list to Turkey so you wouldn't know about it, but you came in when I was doing it and I freaked out and jumped behind the couch."

"Because you wrote a list of awkward things about me?" I asked.

"Yeah, man. I didn't want you to find out."

I nodded. His story made sense, at least to me. Other people might have chosen to perhaps fold the list up and place it in an out of sight location, perhaps a pocket, but not him. When it comes to enthusiasm and determination, he is head and shoulders above the rest, and he is nearly as good as I am at spinning a tale of pure nonsense. But good sense and problem solving? He was about as adept as a concrete mixing truck in those areas.

"That sounds remarkably similar to my day," I said. "I stopped by Emily's place, you see."

"You what?" Travis seemed to swell a bit.

"Now, now, don't worry yourself. I wasn't there to see her," I reassured him.

"Then what, dude?"

"I went there for, uh, a personal errand. Her roommate let me in. It's not like I was sneaking."

"You wanted to sneak in?"

"No, not at all. Like I said, it was a personal errand. But then Emily came home, and I wound up behind her couch and in her fireplace. Did you know she keeps a sofa in front of a fireplace? It's the strangest thing."

"Bro, that's messed up," Travis said. His demeanor had grown chilly, much different from a moment ago when he was all apologies.

"What's that?" I asked, startled at his sudden change.

"Sneaking into Emily's place, dude. How could you do that?"

"You snuck into my place!"

"Your roommate let me in!"

"So did hers for me. It's exactly the same thing."

"Yeah, but you, like, hid out and stuff."

"And you did here too."

Travis pondered. My patient rebuttals seemed to have him stymied. "Yeah, but, like, you did it weird and stuff." He finally said.

"Yes, I recognize the point you are endeavoring to make, but it's not as if no men are ever there. She does have a male roommate."

Travis looked at me in shock. "What? Are you kidding? That's so weird."

I looked at him. Travis was normally very stable in his emotional responses, but today he seemed to be all over the place. At the moment he was registering anxiety, if my eye did not deceive me. "I confess I find myself surprised," I said to him. "I would have thought you worldlier than that. It's not an uncommon practice these days, you know."

"I don't know, I feel like it's kind of strange, you know? I mean it's fine if she does it, I guess, it just makes me feel weird knowing about it. Like, do they ever, I don't know, talk to each other?"

"I presume so. It's quite difficult to coexist in a space without speaking to the other person. Why, take me and James for example. One could hardly keep us from chewing the fat at all hours of the day."

"But what if they started dating or something?"

"I assure you, that won't happen. I can't imagine a person who would want to date the fellow she lives with. But even if they did, they're adults, aren't they? Who are we to say what they should and shouldn't do with each other."

Travis scratched his head. "Yeah, I guess. I just don't know if this girl might be too much for me, you know? Like, I keep finding out new things about her and it just makes me feel like there's no way."

I shrugged. "Could be. It seems that Emily has hidden depths when you look closely. On the surface she appears all sweetness and light, and then you one day discover she has the dark soul of a college professor." I sighed wistfully.

"I guess. Sometimes, Cess, I wonder if we should even be friends. I don't even know what you're saying sometimes."

Saying I was shocked would be putting it lightly. Travis had been tagging about like Mary's little lamb for quite a while now. He seemed to be a permanent addition that I could no more get rid of than my left leg. "Travis, you don't mean to say you wish to end our friendship?" I asked, incredulous.

"No, man, I mean, I don't know. I'm just thinking, you know? Just saying things and wondering. But do you think we seem like we would be friends? I mean, dude, listen to how you talk."

"There is absolutely nothing wrong with the manner in which I speak." I said a little stiffly. "It is full of elegance and, I dare say, a touch of *élan*."

"Yeah dude, I know. I think it sounds weird too. Anyway, I don't know, I guess I just need some time to think about stuff and junk. Maybe you should too. Come on, Turkey."

Travis and his dog exited, and I flopped over on the couch. It was unbelievable to me that Travis would say things like that. I had always imagined us friends, or at least that he thought I was a friend. Coming after the conversation with Violet, it was almost too much to bear. I felt raw and in need of support, but all I seemed to be getting were harsh words.

I took some time to indulge in self-pity. No one

really understood what I was going through. They were all just being mean to me. It isn't easy. Those kinds of thought entertained me for a few minutes before my phone started to vibrate and play *Dancing Queen* by the incomparable band ABBA, which is my preferred ringtone. I leapt to my feet, dug my phone from my pocket, and saw that it was Uncle Gerald calling. That was the last straw, I thought, and I decided I needed to get away.

I quickly leapt into action. First, I pried the back of my phone off and tore the battery out. Then I dashed to my bedroom, flung both phone and battery into my sock drawer, and slammed the drawer shut. Finally, I grabbed some packing tape from my desk and sealed the drawer. I would have a devil of a time getting socks in the immediate future, but that was a small price to pay.

I began to pack a bag, looking wistfully at my sock drawer as I did. I felt it was a certain bet that Uncle Gerald would seek me out, and I did not intend to remain where he could easily find me. The only problem was where to go. I heaved a boulder-sized sigh as I realized there was only one place I could realistically go. And so I set out to Travis's place to attempt to make things right.

CHAPTER 10

Travis lived in Pacific Beach, also known as Land of the Dude. The streets, lined with bars and Mexican food places, are the perfect place to observe the dude-bro or dude-girl in his or her natural habitat. Many people in Southern California consider dude to be a gender-neutral term, citing such examples as, "I called my refrigerator dude." I have my doubts about that, personally.

The actual duplex Travis lived in was several blocks outside of the main drag, tucked on a narrow street. I felt a bit sheepish as I approached the door. It's rather difficult when you have to beg a friend who just questioned your friendship to let you stay with him. It was with some trepidation that I knocked on the door, and when it opened I was shocked to behold Violet there, looking once more her perfectly manicured self.

"Hello Haverford," she said.

I gaped at her in confusion. I looked around to make sure I had, in fact, come to the correct location.

"Travis isn't here right now. He'll probably get back soon. I assume you're here to see him," Violet said.

I finally found my tongue. "How do you know Travis? Why are you here? How did you get in? What's going on?" I found myself gasping as I let loose the questions bouncing around in my mind.

Violet, as befitting her nature, remained cool and collected as she answered. "I met Travis last month when I saved his dog from choking. I come here sometimes to play video games with him. I came in through the door, though now I'm wondering if that's too pedestrian and I should try coming in through the window next time. I'm waiting for Travis to get back. What's going on with you?"

Though I often find Violet maddening in her quest to improve me, I must admit that her outward placidity in times of turmoil is always able to calm my jangled nerves and restore peace to the mind. My pulse slowed to a more regular rhythm and my limbs ceased quavering. There were a lot of thoughts swirling through my mind, ranging from why Violet seemed like she was being so nice right now, to how I managed to get here before Travis. One thing stuck out for some reason, and I grasped at it like a brass ring on an old-fashioned carousel.

"You play video games?" I was surprised at my choice of question, considering everything else going on. Probably it shows something or other about human nature, but you'd have to consult an expert on that.

She smiled at me, a surprisingly genuine smile. "I only started playing them in the last year or so, but I really like them."

Having gotten such a favorable response, I decided to continue with this line of questioning. "Well then, what do you enjoy playing?" I asked.

"*Hyper Newt Farmer.*"

I wasn't certain what I was expecting her to say, not being savvy to the ins and outs of the video game subculture, but that was still a surprise. The collection of words which fell from Violet's mouth, since they could hardly be called a title of any sensible work, exceeded even my wildest imaginings. I was stunned for a moment, hardly daring to ask more for fear of what knowledge I might gain. However, when a person has just told you that their favorite video game is something called *Hyper Newt Farmer*, there are certain questions which must be asked.

I began with one of the simpler ones. "Does this game, by any chance, involve newts?"

Violet grinned indulgently at me. "That's right. There are newts in it."

"I see. Are you in some way responsible for the life of newts?"

"I guess you could say that. In a way."

"So there's more to this game then? Beyond the rearing of the newts? Is it some sort of enforced virtual newt breeding program?"

Violet wrinkled her nose and looked at me disapprovingly. "Absolutely not. She farms."

"Who farms?"

"The newt."

I leaned back and attempted to absorb this piece of information. It was impossible. It was absolutely indigestible, so I didn't even try. "Well, I'm glad to have learned of this," I said, rising to leave. If Violet was going to stay here all evening and talk to me about newts, I would go sleep on the beach and decide what to do in the morning. "Goodbye, Violet."

"Sit down, Haverford," she said. All of her previous chumminess had disappeared like a sheep's coat after a visit to the shearer, and she suddenly seemed a completely different animal. "Now that you're here, I'm going to keep you from getting into trouble again. So what else do you want to know about *Hyper Newt Farmer*?"

I groaned as I sank down to one of the chairs. "Please, anything but that," I said.

"Okay, then let's talk about what you can do to become a more responsible, more compassionate, and all around more pleasant person."

I sighed. "Tell me about *Hyper Newt Farmer*."

I have heard Violet wax poetic, though in her case I suppose it would be technical, about a great variety of dull subjects, but none were duller than the topic of *Hyper Newt Farmer* game design. So dull was her recitation, in fact, that I actually found interest in the feeling of my eyes going glassy. It was a feeling which originated in the back of my eyes, very slowly creeping forward. Then all of the sudden the feeling leapt forward, and my eyes were unfocused marbles. I began attempting to strike the perfect mouth gape, and suffice to say it was with no small dab of relief that, twenty minutes after Violet had begun talking, I was startled to full awareness by Travis and Turkey crashing through the doorway.

"Hey Vi, you here?" Travis called. He was out of sight from the living room, and from the sound of it was either removing his shoes or practicing a hammer toss. Having received an affirmative reply from Violet, he went on. "Sorry I'm late, Turkey needed a run and then there was this dude on a pogo with a lizard and—" his run-on spew of storytelling ceased suddenly when he entered the living room and saw me there. "Oh, what's up bro? I mean not bro. I mean bro." He was clearly rattled.

"Hello Travis." It came out a bit hoarse, and I cleared my throat. "I know you said you needed some time to think, but there are some rather extenuating circumstances… that…" I trailed off as I noticed Violet looking at me with intense interest.

"Don't mind me," she said. "Please, continue. What remarkable thing happened to make Travis need to think?"

"Travis, would there be someplace we could discuss this in private?"

He shrugged. "I guess we could go to the backyard," he said, and shuffled towards a door on the far side of the room. I followed him and found myself in an alley.

"I don't think this is what is normally called a backyard," I said, looking around.

"No, not the alley, dude. Right here." He indicated where he meant.

"Travis, that's a sandbox." It really could be called nothing else. It was a four-feet by two-feet rectangle of short wooden walls filled with sand, with two folding chairs stuck in. It was nearly the saddest thing I had ever heard called a backyard, and to attach that label to it was an act of madness, in my opinion.

"This is totally a backyard, dude," Travis insisted. "The landlord said it was. He was like, it's a piece of the beach at home."

"Your landlord said that?"

Travis shrugged. "Maybe the dude next door

said it. Who cares?"

I sat in one folding chair and Travis sat in the other. "We'll leave that for now. I must speak to you about a serious matter."

"Dude, we just did that. I can't take it now. I just want to go chill with some games and lose big to Vi."

"Really? I recall you bragging now and then of your prowess at video games. Is she really all that good?"

Travis looked at me straight in the eye, in a way which suggested what he was about to say was of the utmost importance. I duly took notice, straightening myself upright from my slightly slouched position. "Bro, she is a straight-up ruthless face stomper."

I crossed a thoughtful leg as I pondered this surprising new piece of information. Violet the ruthless video game face stomper was a whole new Violet I had to take a moment to get used to. On reflection it made sense given the incredibly detailed nature of her lecture on *Hyper Newt Farmer.* It had just been so boring to me I hadn't noticed.

"Well, well," I said aloud, for lack of anything better to say.

"Yeah, you say that, but don't do it when you're gaming, bro. She'll snipe your butt with a turtle shell like that." He snapped his fingers.

"A turtle shell, you say?" I uncrossed the first thoughtful leg and crossed a second one. "Well, well."

"Yeah, dude."

A deep, comfortable silence settled over us as we both considered the intricacies of Violet clobbering us with digital turtle shells. Suddenly I remembered my purpose in being there. "Travis, I need to ask you for a favor."

"Huh? What?"

"A favor, Travis. Might I stay here for a couple of nights?"

"What, like here, here?" he pointed down.

"No, not in the sandbox. Okay fine, I mean backyard. No, your apartment. You see, I'm in a bit of a spot…"

"Sure, no problem."

"What? You mean just like that?"

He shrugged. "I guess. Why not?"

"Well, don't we have to settle our differences first? You know, how you said maybe we shouldn't be friends and stormed out of my apartment?"

"Oh yeah. So what do we do?"

"Well, I'm not sure," I admitted.

We sat another moment in silence, this time thinking about how to breach the gap between us. It was Travis who broke the silence this time. "I know! I saw it in a movie. Two bros were like, aw you suck to each other, and then they punched each other and it was all cool." He stood up. "C'mon bro, punch me."

I stood as well, all my senses tingling with danger. "What? No!"

"Okay, then I will." He reached for me and I ducked away just in the nick of time.

"Travis, we're not going to punch each other. Look at us. You're built like a truck, and I'm more along the lines of a limp noodle. This wouldn't be an even exchange at all."

"Yeah I guess," he said, scratching his head. "Sorry bro. What if we, like, pretended to punch each other? Or is that dumb?"

"That's actually a brilliant idea. We can

compete at a video game, and that will settle things."

Travis nodded. "Oh, but one more thing," he said. "Let's just not talk about Em anymore. I don't think I'm gonna date her, but it would be weird if you talked about it."

I smiled. "Do not worry, Travis. I am going to avoid dating her as well. But I swear on my honor as a Haverford, we won't discuss her anymore." We shook hands and went back in.

"Everything good?" Violet asked us as we settled in the living room.

Travis smiled and nodded. "Yeah, we're gonna play some *Legally Distinct Kart Racing.*"

"Impressive vocabulary, Travis. Please explain," I said.

Travis switched the smile to me. "There's a bunch of games where you race around a track in go-karts and toss junk at each other. They all rip each other off, and they're all the same, so Vi started calling them all *Legally Distinct Kart Racing.*"

"There's another name we sometimes call these games," Violet said to me with a wicked grin as she picked up a control device. "*The Friend Breakers.*"

CHAPTER 11

It was after noon the next day when Travis and Violet began speaking to me again.

"I can't believe you used the banana trick," was the first thing Travis said to me.

"It was just beginner's luck," Violet said as she flipped her hair dismissively.

What had happened was this: I put on an exemplary show of skill, quick thinking, and reflex, with the result that I won the first race, despite the incessant hail of bombs, vegetables, and tar traps that my opponents threw at me. This made both Violet and Travis irritable, and the accusations of banana tricking and beginner's luck started. By the time I had won my forty-sixth consecutive race, they had gone from irritable to downright nasty.

I tried again to explain this to them, but they were having none of it.

"Bro, I know the banana trick when I see it," Travis said. "That was the banana trick."

I sighed wearily. "But think, Travis, how could

I do this banana trick? I don't even know what a banana trick is!"

"Come on, dude, we all saw the banana trick. You saw it, I saw it, and Vi saw it. There you were, with the banana, being all tricky."

"The banana trick is a myth," Violet snapped. "It doesn't exist. He was just lucky. That's all there is to it. If he played today he would be mediocre."

Travis was fuming. "You did not just tell me the banana trick isn't real. You know it is! We even made a pact to never use it 'cuz it's too unfair."

"First of all, I agreed to that dumb pact because you wouldn't shut up about it. Second, can you actually explain to me, right now and in clear terms, how to do the banana trick?"

"What, you don't actually know the banana trick? I'm not telling then. It's, like, too tempting, you know?"

Violet gave him her most serious look. "I'll give you fifty dollars if you tell me and it actually works."

Travis leapt over to the TV and turned his game console on. "Okay, see, you gotta get the banana item, right? Then you're driving along, and you—"

I found their conversation dull and incomprehensible, and it could and probably did continue for some time. I can't say for certain since I chose that moment to leave. There they were, arguing about imaginary bananas with Cecil Haverford present, and then suddenly they were doing it without Cecil Haverford present. From their perspective I would be as a phantom who dissolves through a wall without a trace. In actuality I scooped a spare key from the table next to the door and exited as any sensible corporeal being would.

Once out I was at a bit of a loss as to what to do. I moved down the street with a sort of indecisive lurch, found myself at my car, got in, and began puttering around at random, taking this turn or that as the whim struck me. Eventually I found myself in the region of Balboa Park, one of my favorite locations. I decided to stop there for a bit and take a stroll, beginning with the rose garden.

I have heard that the roses have a period of peak bloom which lasts nearly two months, though I have my suspicions about this. When I personally visit, no matter the time of year, I will have just missed it by a few weeks. It is the most baffling phenomenon I have ever encountered.

This time was no exception. Over half of the bushes were missing their blooms, and the ones that had them were beginning to wilt. I am by no means attempting to imply that the roses are poorly taken care of. On the contrary, keeping so many rose bushes alive and thriving in the desert is a feat which takes careful planning, inhuman diligence, and a touch of divine intervention.

I wandered along the concentric circles of bushes, stopping here to admire a cluster of pink and red flowers that were called something like Passion Fireworks, and stopping there to sniff some yellow blooms which I believe were named Amy Schumer. I was feeling a sense of relaxation and peace that I hadn't felt in quite a while. This is what I believe life is all about, being able to stop and smell the flowers, whether figurative or literal, no matter what they happen to be called. Given this state of mind, you can imagine I was quite jarred when I walked into the pavilion at the center of the garden and tripped over

James's legs.

"Cecil, are you alright?" James cried as he rose from the bench he was perched on. He grabbed my arm and pulled me to my feet.

"James, what are you doing sitting there with those stilts you call legs dangling out in the walkway?" I looked him over. "Why are you wearing a suit?"

He looked at the ground in what appeared to be embarrassment. "I'm meeting someone," he said. "For, you know, a date."

"Wonderful news, to be sure. But James, you do know you're at a park, right? This is not a Michelin Star restaurant."

James gaped at me. "Do you think I'm overdressed? I wanted to make a good impression."

"You are definitely overdressed, but worry not, old chum, I have the solution. Remove your jacket and your tie." He did so, and I took them, donning the jacket and stuffing the tie in one of the pockets. "Now roll up your sleeves."

"That's going to wrinkle them," James objected, but he dutifully did as requested. I gave him an appraising glance.

"No, that's not quite right. You look like a used car salesman. Those pants are all wrong. You need something more casual. Here, switch with me."

"What?" James looked in shock as I started removing my jeans.

"Hurry, before someone comes."

If you ever have a friend or associate with whom you feel you need to forge a stronger bond with, I would highly suggest swapping pants in a pavilion surrounded by rose bushes which are a bit past their prime. I hadn't felt that close to a person since the second grade when William Meyers and I became spit brothers. The look in James's eye, a sort of bewildered awe, told me that he felt the same.

"I need my belt," he mumbled.

He was certainly thin as a rail. I had some trouble squeezing his pants closed. I passed him the belt and took in the completed look. "You're perfect," I declared. "I'll run along now and let you get on with your waiting. I trust she isn't late?"

"Bye, Cecil," James said with a certain pointedness. I smiled indulgently. Nerves must be getting to him, and me mentioning his date being late probably only exacerbated that feeling. I waved a cheery goodbye and scurried over to the pedestrian bridge crossing the road which separated the rose garden from the main area of Balboa Park.

I felt a warm feeling from helping a pal. Even with my own troubles looming, it was wonderful that I could still bring some light and joy to another person's life. I turned around in the middle of the bridge to see if I could spot James, but the roof of the pavilion hid him from my view. I shrugged, turned back to continue on my way, and nearly knocked Emily to the ground.

"Emily, are you okay?" I asked. "What a surprise seeing you here."

"Oh no, it's my fault," she said. "I was sneaking up on you. I thought you were someone else." She cast her gaze downwards as she said it, almost like she was embarrassed. I wondered at running into two people who were so embarrassed within minutes of each other.

"Ah, I see." I looked at the ground as well. It suddenly seemed difficult to know what to say to her. I didn't want to seem too friendly, but it wouldn't do to completely snub her either. We stood in silence for a moment, shuffling our feet while deciding what to say.

She managed to break the silence first. "Is that a new suit?"

"Oh, yes," I said. "Or, rather, it's borrowed. I wanted something to stroll around the park in, you know?"

I braced myself against the railing as she laughed. "Do you often borrow suits to walk around the park in?"

"Oh, certainly," I lied for some reason. "It makes one feel quite dapper and in charge, you know? Like you have a certain English stiff-upper-lip-ness to you." I had slipped into a faux accent which, truth be told, had equal parts British, New Zealand, and American Midwest to it.

She laughed again, this time with much less pep to it. "I need to be going now," she said. "I'm meeting someone and I'm already late."

I was relieved, to be honest. I felt our conversation had thus far struck the right balance of friendly and don't come closer, but I was worried how much longer that could last. I realized as she left that she hadn't said anything about the letter she received. I felt agitated just thinking about it, and I hurried along to take in the sights and calm myself.

Fortunately for me, Balboa Park is full of calming sights. The big fountain right when you step off the pedestrian bridge is one of my favorites, and I enjoyed the sight for a few minutes. I stopped at the large reflecting pond near the botanical garden, which reflected nothing of note, and gazed at the koi which lived there. I was already starting to feel relaxed again.

I discovered as I wandered more that the suit actually was making me feel dapper and in charge. I suddenly understood why James wore them so much. I strutted past the outdoor organ without a care in the world and was even tempted to go into the Japanese garden, but I decided against it; I have a general policy of never paying to enter a garden.

Within a half hour I was feeling as cheerful and upbeat as an oyster in muck. I headed over to one of the little-known gems the park has to offer: a hidden cactus garden tucked away behind some building or other. The plants there all were of the type that looked strange and alien, and no one was ever there, so I could count on being alone with my thoughts.

As I rounded the corner, I saw this wouldn't be the case this time. A couple was there, consisting of a tall, gawky looking man and a pint-sized woman with red, curly hair. I realized with a start that it was James and Emily. They were standing together awkwardly, looking at the cacti. Emily seemed to say something which caused James to turn to her. Suddenly she grabbed him by the collar and hauled him down to plant quite an extended kiss on him.

The world swirled around the pair as I watched. I couldn't believe what I was seeing. Emily and James being together like that was a shock to the system. My first impulse was to rush over and congratulate them, but I didn't know if this was the right time. Then I became horrified at James's kissing technique. I decided I needed some time to process this.

I hurried back to my car. If Emily was with James, that meant there was no way she would have designs on me. Unless she had one of those fickle hearts which grows weary of men at the drop of a hat. But if that was the case, then would she even be interested in me for the long term? I knew I had to get some outside advice on this matter, and the first person I thought of to ask was Violet.

I sped my way back to Travis's home. With any luck Violet would still be there. At the very least Travis might know where she would be.

I found a spot for my car on the street, walked a couple of blocks to Travis's building, and used the key I had taken earlier. I swung the door open and was greeted by the sight of Violet and Travis on the couch, half-undressed and in a very intimate position. I leapt back in surprise, upset the table next to the door, and went crashing to the floor with it.

CHAPTER 12

"How long has this been going on?" I asked. Violet and Travis were fully dressed once more and the furniture I had disturbed was righted again. I was sporting a few bruises, but nothing that looked too bad. I felt I had taken more of a mental battering than a physical one.

Violet looked at me with cool composure. Not once had she seemed embarrassed. Travis, in contrast, was still bright red, and he looked like he wanted me to leave. Both of them regarded me silently.

"Well?" I persisted. "What do you have to say for yourselves?"

"Why are you wearing a suit?" Violet asked me.

I looked down at myself. I had forgotten about that, what with everything else going on. "That's not important right now."

"It doesn't look like it fits very well."

"I said it's not important!" I was fuming, but I couldn't help myself. "Tell me, how long have you two been…" I made vague hand gestures, attempting to get my meaning across.

"Dude, what?" Travis said. Violet waved her hand, indicating she would take the lead.

"I told you how we met. It started a few weeks after that."

"Vi!" Travis exclaimed. "That's so not cool, dude. I don't want him knowing that."

"What does it matter?" she said. "We're both adults, attractive, and a bit lonely. We're allowed to…" she mimicked my hand gestures.

"See, that's the kind of thing I don't want Cess hearing." He turned to me. "I'm not lonely, dude. I've got loads of friends. So many friends, dude, I can't even hang with them most of the time. You know why? Because I'd rather hang with you, bro."

I was still fuming. My face felt hot and my pulse was elevated. "Travis, I'm not concerned with whether you're lonely or not," I said, trying to keep my cool.

"Not lonely," he said.

My voice tightened. "I'm concerned with you carrying on in this way while dating Emily."

Violet looked mildly surprised. "Oh, were you dating Emily?" she asked.

"Man, see, I didn't want this either," Travis complained. "This sucks."

"You didn't want me to know about you dating someone? That wasn't our agreement."

"You had an agreement about this?" I asked.

Violet turned back to me. "We did. Who wouldn't have an agreement when entering into this sort of arrangement? We wouldn't want either of us to have hurt feelings." She looked at Travis. "Except you did not abide by our terms, and now I'm dangerously close to having hurt feelings. Imagine, finding out the man you're hooking up with wants to date your new friend."

It was Travis's turn to look surprised. "Wait, you know Emily?"

I smiled. "Now everyone's secrets are coming out," I said.

"It's no secret," Violet said. "I didn't think Travis would know her. Why would he?" She thought a second. "So, are you going to continue seeing her?"

Travis scowled. "No, I don't really think there was a connection there."

Violet grunted. "Meaning you couldn't have sex with her," she said.

Travis's scowl deepened. "No, I didn't forget that part of our deal. And I was trying what you told me about."

I don't always have the quickest of minds, but on occasion I will put two and two together in a split second and see the deeper meaning behind what someone is saying. It's like when you look at one of those pictures of wavy lines and colors and see something that might be a dog or a boat in it, only this made actual sense. "You're the one who told him about Christian Dating!" I cried.

Violet grinned at me. "It was mostly a joke."

As I watched Travis blush again, I felt a wave of weakness spread over me. My face still felt hot and I was starting to get a little dizzy. "I'm leaving," I said suddenly.

Travis looked relieved, but when Violet looked at me she seemed concerned. "Are you okay?" she asked.

"I need to go home," I said. "Maybe lie down for a while."

My friends made appropriate farewells, but I didn't pay much attention as I wobbled to the door and on out. From there I hazily made my way back to my car and then puttered back to my apartment.

James was there when I arrived, and he looked at me with shock on his face. I must have appeared unwell. I vaguely heard him inquire about my condition, but I just could not focus enough to reply. Instead I teetered into my room and collapsed on my bed.

Sometimes when a sickness comes on quickly it leaves quickly. In this case it lingered on for nearly a week. I could barely get out of my bed the first few days, which made taking care of myself quite a challenge. James assisted when he could, but he had to work during the day. His unusually strong aversion to getting sick prevented him from doing much when he was around. His heart was in the right place, but he was no caretaker. In fact, his desire to remain healthy was so strong he barred me from leaving my room while he was home and made me promise my excursions outside when he wasn't around would be quick and involve touching as few surfaces as possible. It was the first time I had experienced him really putting his foot down about anything.

All of this is to explain why I didn't know about Washington Irving until I was better.

I woke in the evening from a refreshingly long nap with the feeling of health vibrating through my body once again. I left my room, anticipating James's complaint.

"It's okay, I feel fine once again," I said.

"Are you sure? What if you're still contagious?" He asked, putting himself behind the kitchen counter.

I waved a dismissive hand. "Not at all, I am fit and hale." I took in a deep breath to demonstrate how healthy I was, but it turned into a wheeze when I noticed Washington Irving sitting on the counter near James.

"That doesn't sound fit and hale to me," James said.

"What is he doing here?" I cried, pointing.

"Your uncle left him here." James picked Washington Irving up and scratched him under the chin. "Who's a good kitty?"

"Uncle Gerald was here? How did I miss this vital piece of information?"

"You had a high fever and were completely out of it. I think he came to talk to you, but after taking one look he said you could use your rest. Then he asked if we would watch his cat."

I groaned. "And you went ahead and said yes? James, this is a ploy of his. Now I shall have to return the blasted thing to him. He will have me at his abode, and I will be required to fully attend to whatever he says."

"It might be worthwhile listening to him," James said. "He can give good advice, you know. He gave me some career advice while he was here."

"Let me guess, he said you should be less diffident."

"He didn't use that exact word, but I suppose that's what it amounted to."

I laughed hollowly. It seemed unfortunate for James, who was not versed in Uncle Gerald's ways, to be so taken in by him. "He says that to everyone. In his mind the whole of the world is lazy, and he is the only one even trying to do any work."

"He is an exceptional person," James said, his voice getting heated. "I think it's good to hear what he has to say and try to follow his advice. I intend to, but…" he finished with a wistful sigh.

My brain leapt into action once again, sifting through recent events to place why that sigh was so wistful. It was on a roll lately, accomplishing this task twice in the space of a week, and I felt very proud of myself as I asked, "How did your date last week fare?"

James looked startled. He demurred a bit, then said "I suppose the date itself went well."

"Then why the long face?"

"It's not the date itself but the afterwards, you know? I mean the follow up. I know I'm supposed to wait a certain amount of days before calling her, but after waiting a few days it was difficult to get up the courage to do it. I kept thinking about whether she even still remembered how nice the date was or if she still liked me at all. Every time I tried to pick up my phone and call her, I had such anxiety I felt like I was going to be sick."

"James, what are you telling me?" I said, stricken.

"I haven't spoken to her in a week," he said sheepishly.

I wobbled like a drunken top, nearly treading on Washington Irving as I did. It felt like James was the one thing between me and a future bound to a college professor, or at any rate an aspiring one. I found myself in the rare position of agreeing with Uncle Gerald.

"James, perhaps you are right about Uncle Gerald," I said. "Maybe we both need to be less diffident and more deliberate in our actions."

"Do you think so? But how will I manage it? I think it's been too long now for me to call her."

Privately I agreed with him, but I felt determined to not give up without a fight. "Don't worry, chum. I'm sure you can work through any initial unpleasantness and once more be two hearts united as one."

"We only had one date."

"Nonsense, you are fully two hearts as one."

"Cecil, you don't even know who she is."

He was right that I wasn't supposed to know who she was. It can be tricky sometimes to keep those kinds of details straight. I congratulated myself briefly on not saying Emily's name. "It's just a feeling I have. Trust me, you'll be fine."

James sighed. "I hope so. And how are you overcoming your diffidence?"

It hadn't occurred to me that I would actually do anything, but I saw that I had to come up with something quickly. "I'll go talk to Uncle Gerald tomorrow," I said, then instantly regretted it.

James nodded. "I guess that's doing something you're not looking forward to. It's a deal."

I smiled and felt suddenly tired at the thought of having to not only drive to LA, but also have what might be an all-day session with Uncle Gerald. I excused myself to go to bed. Washington Irving followed me in, jumped on my bed, and sat licking himself with the smugness that only a cat can possess.

CHAPTER 13

I was brooding as I drove north to Los Angeles, while Washington Irving snoozed in his cat carrier. I couldn't help but imagine the danger to myself if James did not get in touch with Emily and mollify any hurt feelings his lack of communication had caused. A person will wait a reasonable amount of time for gold, but eventually they will see it's not in the cards and decide that silver will do just as well. That is to say, I imagined Emily would decide James is a raw deal and link her lot with me.

For a moment I cursed James's name, but I decided that would not do. He was a friend, and friends do not curse each others' names. I decided to curse no one in particular, and instead spent the rest of the trip to Uncle Gerald's fruitlessly trying to come up with a plan. It was difficult because I knew I had messed up his plan for me at every turn. It seemed impossible that I would be able to follow any plan at all. I eventually settled on throwing myself at his mercy and hoping for the best.

Uncle Gerald did not actually live in Los Angeles proper. He resided in the Hills area of Manhattan Beach, a suburb located on the coast south of LA. Manhattan Beach is notable for having very narrow one-way streets, though the impression I always get is that everyone drives two ways on them anyway. The Hills, being the more opulent area, is the exception. The city splurged on a center dividing line, which I would estimate a full fifty percent of people noticed.

The neighborhood he lived in was filled with homes which weren't quite mansions, but definitely aspired to be. They all overlooked what would be a fairly nice ocean view if it weren't for all the other homes jostling for viewing space. This isn't to say it's not a fine place, but it does feel crowded.

I turned away from that almost pleasant view and faced Uncle Gerald's house, an ultra-modern thing which was somewhat larger than its neighbors. James and Emily still weighed heavily on my mind, but now I had to focus on what Uncle Gerald would say to me. I reached into my car, dragged the cat carrier out, toddled up to the door, and knocked. Uncle Ted and his permed fluff of hair opened up and greeted me.

Uncle Ted had once been a fierce captain of industry. I have never been clear on exactly what it was he dealt in, something about widgets or investments, but he had ended up with a substantial pile of money and a severe indigestion complaint because of it. He probably would have kept on going with his business until his dying day, accumulating more money and perhaps a stomach ulcer, but one night he had a life-changing experience. While suffering from insomnia caused by a particularly acute bout of heartburn, he saw an episode of The Joy of Painting, hosted by Bob Ross.

Uncle Ted had never seen or heard anyone like Bob Ross before. Here was a person who was wholly dedicated to creating beauty, who assured him that there were no mistakes, only happy accidents. "It's time to make a big decision," Ross said, and Uncle Ted, in his sleep-deprived, pain-addled state, knew that those softly spoken words were meant just for him. "It's your world."

The next day Uncle Ted made one of the most substantial decisions of his life. He announced his retirement, started the process of selling his business, then threw himself into living the ideal Rossian lifestyle with the same gusto with which he made his millions. Unfortunately, his temperament made him completely miss the point of what Ross had said. He painted somewhere around five hundred identical pictures, trying to perfectly emulate one particular painting he had seen on the show. Once he was satisfied, he decided to flex his own creative muscles. Thus far he has painted only about three hundred nearly identical paintings of the semi-ocean view he sees from his second-floor studio, but I firmly believe that he has another couple of hundred attempts left in him.

"Hi there, Cecil," he said, trying as always to make his gravelly voice sound silky and relaxing. "What brings you to our little animal sanctuary?"

"Hello, Uncle Ted." I said cheerily. "Still trying to catch the local squirrels, are you?"

Uncle Ted chuckled. "Those little rascals are quick, but that's no problem. I know they appreciate everything we do for them."

"Undoubtedly." I held up the cat carrier and got to the point. "Uncle Gerald wanted me to visit. I brought Washington Irving back." I patted the cat carrier in my hand.

"Oh, so that's where that little rascal got to." One of the unfortunate aspects of Uncle Ted's obsession with Bob Ross was his tendency to refer to all animals as rascals. Another unfortunate aspect was his desire to talk about animals almost all the time. "Gerald is in the back yard. Let's head over there and we can let this little fella out."

"How is Uncle Gerald doing today?" I asked as we walked. I kept my tone conversational, but I was desperate for this piece of intelligence. At this moment, in my mind, life and death hung in the balance.

As usual, Uncle Ted was not very helpful. "Same as always," he said, then his face lit up. "Have I ever told you how we met?"

"Yes, actually, many times," I said, trying to prevent another retelling.

"I was a struggling businessman, just started my own company," he began, ignoring me. "Your Uncle Gerald was my legal advisor, but what he really wanted to do was teach."

I shuddered. "Yes, yes. Since this is what we're doing, let's keep it moving, shall we?"

"Alright, alright, just give me a second. So there was this property, you see, and everyone thought it was just a terrible property. No potential in it at all. But your Uncle Gerald told me about some sort of legal loophole that would let us develop a strip mall, right smack dab in the middle of a suburb!" For a moment the old businessman gleam shone in his eyes. "Well, you know what happened to our competition, don't you?" He started chuckling at what he was about to say.

I rolled my eyes. "You beat the devil out of

them."

"We beat the devil out of them!" he hooted.

"Fascinating, Uncle Ted, but as usual that was all about business. You never speak of the heart when you tell that story. Not that I can blame you, having married Uncle Gerald."

"Well shoot, we were such good business partners, of course we married. Marriage is the biggest and best merger of them all. It wasn't until after the business was sold that we married, but we were together before that all right." He waved a hand dismissively at the past events. "But that's all history. Here we are."

We had arrived at the backyard, which was modestly sized for the house, but still large by most standards. The ground was made of cement with seashells embedded in it, and giant egg-shaped seats woven of wicker were scattered here and there. A three-foot square patch of grass with a tree stuck in it was the only testament to nature. A stark yard, to be sure.

Uncle Gerald was lounging in an eggshell about the size of a bed. As I approached, he was making several deft pen marks on a paper, undoubtedly destroying some poor student's dreams in the process.

"Hello, Uncle Gerald," I said.

"Ah, good, you're here," he said without looking up.

"Yes, I am. I brought Washington Irving." I opened the carrier and let the cat out.

"Wonderful." Uncle Gerald got up, seized Washington Irving, set him on the nearby wall, and let him hop into the neighbor's yard. "That wasn't Washington Irving," he explained. "I borrowed the neighbor's cat because I knew you wouldn't know the difference. For some reason you seem to think every cat you see is Washington Irving. As if I was really going to send my darling little prince to live with you."

I had nothing to say to this. His trickery didn't really surprise me, but I had thought I could recognize Washington Irving when I saw him. I kept a severe silence so as to not give anything away.

"You don't need to look so much like a stuffed frog," he said. "It was just a little joke."

"I'm not looking like a stuffed frog. If you must know, I'm maintaining a proud, stately silence, much like—"

"Then please continue with that silence," he interrupted. "I take back the stuffed frog comment. You're doing a commendable job. But enough pleasantries, I summoned you here for a reason."

I gulped, wondering what sort of evil he might have come up with in the time since we last spoke. What would he say now about the mistakenly sent love letter?

"I'm throwing a party," Uncle Gerald said. "I want you to attend."

Air whooshed out of me as if relief had socked me in the gut. Then I recovered myself. There had to be more to this, I thought.

"That's it?" I asked, feeling suspicious.

"That's it."

"You don't expect me to steal the diamonds off someone's finger while I'm there?"

"No, of course not," he scoffed. "What kind of host would I be if I did that?"

"Certainly not the kind who would just invite his nephew to a party with no ulterior motive. There must be something you want from me."

He sighed as if this were a terrible burden he was suffering under. "Well, if you must know, Robert Updike, the head of HR from Tompkins, Richards, and Armstrong, will be attending. You will apologize for your conduct in his office when you interviewed with him, as well as the asinine letter you sent in place of my well-worded apology. He has assured me he is amenable to such an apology. It's possible, if you show yourself in a good light while he is mollified, you could still have a job there."

"Aha!" I exclaimed. "So the truth comes out. This is all a ploy to get me employed!"

"Don't be ridiculous. This is a charity event. I would never create such an event solely for getting you employment. But that doesn't mean we can't use it to our advantage. That's why we have charity events."

"And here I was thinking it was for charity."

He shrugged. "Why let a good opportunity go to waste?"

I was about to tell him that I would have nothing to do with his plan by saying, "I am not your charity case," a wonderful line I actually thought up right on the spot, if you can believe it. But then I realized I actually was one.

"That sounds like a plan which is, er, sound." I said.

It was Uncle Gerald's turn to be suspicious, and he raised an eyebrow to show it. "Really? Just like that? I expected you to put up more of a fuss."

"I just want to make you happy, Uncle Gerald," I said sweetly. The truth was, I thought I could easily avoid Robert Updike at a crowded event. Furthermore, I had an idea. "I do have one request to make of you in return."

He laughed, delighted. "This has never happened before! So what do you want?"

I smiled, proud of what I had come up with. Emily and James were still in the back of my mind this whole time, and to my surprise I had come up with a clever scheme. If they were invited to Uncle Gerald's party and had some of his good food and drink, then everything would click for them.

"I'd like you to invite some of my friends to your party too."

Uncle Gerald frowned. He could tell something was up, but he couldn't quite figure it out. After a moment he shrugged. "I can't imagine why you would want that, but it's easy enough." He called to Uncle Ted, who all this time had been prowling around muttering things about light and shadows, and waved him over. "Ted, get some invitations please."

Uncle Ted disappeared for a moment, then returned carrying several papers gilded in pink gold. I raised my eyebrows at them. I didn't think Uncle Gerald went for such tackiness.

He saw my look. "We're raising money for breast cancer research," he said, then grinned at me wryly. "You simply must have pink when talking about breast cancer. Society demands it."

I could hardly believe Uncle Gerald was cracking a low-key joke with me. It might be worth it to give in to his demands at times, if this was the attitude he took when I did.

I wrote four invitations, not wanting to leave Violet and Travis out. I wondered at that briefly. I hadn't wanted Violet back in my life, but now that she was, it seemed entirely natural. She wouldn't want to miss a bash like this, and I wanted her to see it. I wasn't sure if Travis would really want to see it, but he would like to be there with Violet since they were… together? I shoved the associated mental image out of my head.

I probably would have been awash in the warm feelings of friendship all the way back to San Diego, but as we were saying goodbye Uncle Gerald gave me a pointed look.

"Don't mess this up," he said with a glint in his eye that reminded me whatever friendliness we had shared, I was still dealing with Uncle Gerald. I gulped, a chill running down my spine. I was firmly committed.

CHAPTER 14

Several days later the invitations arrived at their various destinations. Emily was surprised to get one and called me to say so.

"But why am I invited?" she asked me. "I don't even know your uncles."

I had anticipated this question and had come up with an answer I thought would satisfy her. "I thought it would be a great opportunity for you to meet Uncle Gerald and get some advice for being a college professor."

I held my phone a respectful distance from my head while Emily laughed. "I guess you don't know," she said. "I've decided not to become a professor."

I felt my heart thump. "Excuse me, you what?"

"Yeah, I think I might want to be a writer."

My legs turned to jelly, and I found myself on the floor. This put a new spin on things. If Emily wasn't intent on becoming a college professor, did that mean I should consider her a potential romantic interest again? Or was it too much that she had even considered it? I felt lost and adrift, confused by what my feelings were. "I hope you will still come to my uncle's soiree," I heard myself say.

"Well sure," she said. "It sounds delightful."

After saying goodbye, I set my phone down and had a small case of the shakes. Once those had passed, with my mind still reeling, my body took action. I slipped out the door, down the stairs, and scooted over to the apartment mailboxes. I opened the one shared by James and myself, pulled out the envelopes it contained, and saw the one I was looking for: small, off-white, and gilded in pink-gold.

I scurried behind the building, casting furtive glances around me. No one was around. I made for the dumpsters and flung the envelope in, then stood for a moment rubbing my clammy hands together. I shook my head and returned to my apartment.

When I got back my phone was ringing. It was Travis, calling me to express excitement over going to, and I quote, "One of those parties with the teeny hot dogs on a tray." I reminded him to dress appropriately, and when I hung up, I was confident there was only a fifty percent chance he would show up in shorts.

I had barely put down my phone when it started ringing again. It was Violet this time, thanking me for getting her an invitation to my uncle's event. I told her it wasn't a problem, then I hesitated for a moment.

"Violet, you've known me for some time now," I said, and she acknowledged it. "Am I a bad friend?"

"You have the capacity to be a bad friend, yes," she said.

"But I can be a good friend?"

"You can be all right sometimes."

After saying goodbye, I contemplated my choices. I felt like I'd had a string of failures recently. The question was whether I wanted to fail James as a friend also, and when I put it to myself like that, it seemed clear what to do.

As luck would have it, James arrived home just at that moment, looking dashingly morose, if that's a way someone can look.

"What's wrong, old pal?" I asked, concerned by the way the shadows gathered under his eyes.

He heaved a sigh to end all sighs and flopped down on our couch. "I finally worked up the nerve to talk to Emily, and it didn't go well."

"She snubbed you, did she?"

He made an affirmative noise, and I shook my head, feeling compassion for him. Fortunately, I had just the thing to cheer him up.

"James, my Uncle Gerald is throwing a bash, and you're invited."

He buried his face in a pillow and made a moan.

"Now don't be like that," I said. "This is a great opportunity. You see, Emily will be in attendance. All you need to do is go up to her and speak a few romantic words. Before you know it, everything will be hunky dory, as they say."

James sat up. "Who says that?" he asked.

"James, this isn't the time to be arguing semantics," I said. "This is a serious matter."

"Why would Emily be at a party your uncle is having?"

"Because I got her invited, and I got you invited." I paused. "But your invitation got lost in the mail," I said, hoping I didn't sound wooden and hollow.

"What did you do to the invitation?" he asked in a way which told me the jig was up.

I groaned. "I threw it away because Emily said she didn't want to be a college professor anymore, but then I thought better of it because you're my friend and I want to be a good friend to you. So she's all yours, chum."

James stood up. "Cecil, she's a person, not something to be given to prove what a good friend you are. It's her decision."

I nodded. "Indeed. So are you going to the party?"

"Yes!" he shouted as he stomped to his room.

When the day of the party came, James's mood was still in the dumps. It was a rather morose trip up to Manhattan Beach with him, and for once I felt glad to be arriving at Uncle Gerald's home. As we ambled to the door, James suddenly started swaying like a palm tree in a hurricane.

"Cecil is that Emily?" he asked, pointing her out as she entered the house.

"Yes, I believe so." I looked at him. "Why are you so shocked? I said she would be here."

"I didn't believe you! Now what am I going to do?"

I felt a growing impatience, but I pushed it down. "Why, go talk to her. That was the plan."

James gave me a sort of goggle-eyed look for a moment, then nodded slowly. "Yes Cecil, I think I do have something I can tell her," he said.

"Wonderful! Then let's go in and you can get to work."

We knocked on the door and were let in by

some manner of hired help. The hired help then led us to the living room, which had been rearranged into something I might call a cocktail party room. It was festooned with pink and white streamers and more than spacious enough to comfortably house the approximately forty people milling about in it. Drink tables in the appropriate colors littered the room, and for good measure a bar had been temporarily installed near one wall. It gave me the impression that Uncle Gerald had gone all out in a manner which actually cost him the least time and money possible.

James and I stood for a moment surveying the crowd, then he turned and gave me another pop-eyed look.

"Was that Travis I just saw?" he asked.

"Quite probably it was," I said. I easily picked him out in the sea of sports jackets. The fifty percent had not actually fallen on the side of shorts. Instead, Travis was sporting a white tuxedo with a red ruffled shirt. I turned back to James. "But how do you know Travis? It seems extraordinary that you would know him also."

"He comes to our apartment all the time. Of course I know who he is."

"Right, I had forgotten that. Did you know Violet knows him? It was one of the biggest shocks I'd received in quite some time."

"Who's Violet?"

"Please James, you went on a date with her."

James blushed a little. "I forgot. I was, um, distracted." He tugged at his collar. "I should go find Emily."

I was staring at Travis as he tried to high five a man who looked like he was at least a hundred, but I turned back when James said that. "Are you sure you're ready? You know what you need to do, right? Think romantic."

James gave me a strange look. "I know what to say."

I walked over to Travis as James left. I was incredibly curious as to what he could be talking to the old man about, and why he was wearing such a gaudy outfit.

"Travis, nice to see you made it," I said as I approached. "What possessed you to wear a tuxedo?"

"Bro, you told me like a thousand times that I should dress nice," he said. "I'm just doing what you said."

"This is true," I conceded. "Sometime we'll discuss the range of options that fall under the category of dressing nice."

"Yeah whatevs. Hey, do you know Earl?" Travis gestured to the elderly man. "He's a really cool dude. You should tell him about how we met. That's a great story!"

I was completely caught off guard by this request. To tell the truth, I could not remember how Travis and I had met. It seemed like he was an eternal feature of my time in San Diego. "Well, we were at the beach, weren't we?" I eventually hazarded. "And then we just met, as I recall."

"No man, you're leaving out all the good stuff. Go on, tell him. I was surfing, right?"

I tugged at my collar a bit. Travis's prompt was of no help, as he seemed to spend at least half of his time at the beach surfing. "Travis, I'm afraid I don't really recall the specifics right now," I admitted. "It was a rather long time ago, you know?"

Travis gaped at me. "Are you kidding me, bro? It's why I call you my best bro! And you just up and forgot?" He drew himself up and looked at me with a haughty gaze, which came across more comical than anything else given what he was wearing. "That's cold, bro," he said and stalked away.

I did a little gaping of my own, opening my mouth, closing it, then opening it again for good measure. I turned to Earl and gave him a helpless look.

"Totally cold, bro," he said and stumped off.

I felt thoroughly off balance, and it wasn't until I had managed to grasp a steadying glass of wine that I felt equal to reviewing what had just happened. Apparently I had once again made some sort of breach of Bro Code, and such a grievous one that even Earl felt compelled to censure me.

I noticed Violet was standing beside me. "Violet, do you remember how we met?" I asked her.

"We were in a human sexuality class together," she said without missing a beat. "You fell asleep and slumped over, resting your head on my shoulder. I shoved you so hard you ended up sprawled in one of the aisles. A month later we met again at a party where you managed to convince me you weren't a creep." She sipped her drink. "You may have regressed since then, unfortunately."

"I think you invented the first part of that story, but never mind. Should I have the right to be angry at you if you forgot how we met?"

Violet shrugged. "I think it would be silly because it has no sentimental meaning to either of us. We met, we got along well enough, we became friends."

"I appreciate that. Can you believe Travis just

got mad at me because I couldn't remember how we met?"

Violet's eyes widened. "Haverford, that's not okay."

I was taken aback. "What do you mean? You just said it doesn't matter."

"No, I said it doesn't matter how you and I met. How you and Travis met is a different matter. I can't believe that you forgot that."

"Well if you're going to get angry at me too, I'll just go somewhere else," I said with what I hoped was a good amount of dignity. Violet waved dismissively as I left.

I decided to inhabit some corner of the room and sulk for a bit, even if it did seem childish, but in my haste to get there I ran into and nearly bowled over Emily. "Oh, I'm very sorry," I said to her.

"Don't worry about it," she said. She looked like a garment that had been vigorously scrubbed on a washing board, but not before it had seen some things. She was drooping, and her eyes were ringed with dark circles. Yes, all the signals of fatigue were certainly there.

"A bit under the weather?" I asked her courteously.

"I'm just tired," she said. "I've had a lot of work to do with classes, I had a couple more terrible dates, and then I saw James here and I got nervous."

I nodded, feeling sympathetic to her plight. Here was a woman who had done nothing wrong, and yet the world was crushing her down. Then I felt like I had missed something and reviewed what she said. "Why are you nervous about seeing James?" I asked.

Emily sighed. "I don't know how he feels

about me. I mean, I think I know. He didn't call me for a while, after all. It's hard to know if he got busy, or if he thought I came on strong and didn't want to date me but then his other dates didn't work out and so he thought maybe he would give it another try. That happens, you know. I may have even done it myself." She ended her whirlwind explanation by looking sheepishly at me.

I felt a strange humming feeling in my head. It seemed the thing to be done was to throw myself at her feet and ask her to run off with me to a foreign land where we could be together forever away from all of this. I wasn't sure what this was we needed to get away from, but it seemed imperative. I felt the pull of base desires against my notions of friendship, and this time friendship won out.

"Are you saying that you would be open to him expressing his love for you here tonight?" I asked.

Emily looked serious. "I don't know if I'd want love just yet. We've only been on one date." She suddenly looked embarrassed as she realized what she said. "Forget I said that! We weren't telling people."

I decided to ignore that. I was probably the only person who would have cared, and I was determined to not care. Instead, I said "Stay here and I'll find James and direct him towards you. Then you two may declare whatever you like to each other, no pressure."

Emily laughed a quiet laugh which caused only two or three heads to turn. "Thanks Cecil. I really appreciate that."

I gulped, the feeling of buzzing in my head returning. It felt like an angry swarm of love hornets. "Oh, I'm not all that great, really," I said.

"No, you're surprisingly nice. Maybe we should hang out again sometime. Like, in a group." She smiled, then suddenly grimaced and rubbed her forehead again. "I have such a headache. It's going to be hard staying through the whole thing."

I felt torn. On the one hand, linking these two sundered souls together once more would be the best for the both of them. On the other hand, the suddenly warm feelings I was having towards Emily made me want her. She had a headache, I thought, so she should be escorted away and maybe wrapped in a comfortable blanket for good measure. After a moment of consideration, I thought a compromise could do well. She should speak to James and then leave. "Don't worry, these shindigs of my uncles' are always a snore," I said. "Why don't you just leave early? Really, you won't miss anything."

Emily began responding, but she was cut off by the din of Uncle Gerald banging a fork against a wine glass. "Everyone, please, may I have your attention," he said. "If you will all kindly follow me to the backyard, we will begin serving dinner."

I felt a sensation as though the ceiling had collapsed on my head. Uncle Gerald had not said anything about this being a dinner party. I realized he did so purposefully, so I would have to speak to Robert Updike. Probably I was seated next to him. I was doomed.

CHAPTER 15

One positive aspect of finding yourself in so many scrapes in such a short period of time is that you begin to take them in stride. What would normally seem like an earth-shattering event now seemed commonplace. Furthermore, I was able to keep my cool and come up with a plan. I decided I had to run for it, but first I had to point James in Emily's direction. "Stay here for a moment," I said to her, and darted off.

James was across the room, hidden behind a few stragglers. "James, this is a dinner party," I said to him.

"Yeah, I think I figured that out." I didn't particularly like his tone, but I decided to ignore it.

"Listen to me carefully. This is your chance." I gripped him by the shoulders to make sure he was paying close attention and pulled him out of the flow of guests on their way to the back yard. "Emily still has feelings for you. She's dying to talk to you."

James did his best fish impression, his mouth opening into a gape and his eyes bulging in surprise.

"Cecil, are you certain?"

I nodded. "Absolutely, straight from the horse's mouth, so to speak. I must prep you though, for things won't necessarily be easy. You see, she has just been talking about maybe dating me again. Also, she has something of a headache."

James's excitement deflated. His mouth closed into a hard line. His eyes returned to their proper size. He went from looking like a fish to looking like a stern, disappointed statue in record time. "I wish you hadn't told me that."

"Nonsense," I said. "Knowing about her headache will enable you to be kind about it. You might offer her a soothing cold compress, or some headache medicine and water. Your options are practically limitless!"

James shook his head slowly, maintaining eye contact. "No, I mean about her wanting to date you. Why would you tell me that?"

"James, really. This is not a problem. I am not going to date Emily." I immediately began thinking about what it would be like if I dated Emily and had to forcibly push those thoughts away. "I'm here for you, and we're going to fix your relationship problems."

"Why even bother trying to fix what you call my relationship problems?"

"Because I'm a good friend!" I all but shouted. "Now, here's what you need to do." My mind had been humming along in the background of this conversation, and it had produced a stunning plan that was sure to smooth over any initial awkwardness when James and Emily first spoke. "Refuse all food at dinner."

"What did you say?" James asked, startled.

I furrowed my brow. "No, wait, I told her to leave before dinner started but after you talked to her. Tell her to stay for dinner, then don't eat a thing."

"I'm hungry you know."

"Good. It will make you look more pitiable. A person who sees her beloved in such agony that he can't even bear to take a bite of food will want to minister to him and soothe his aching brow."

"I thought I was supposed to soothe her brow."

"You can take turns."

"And I'm not her beloved!"

"Nonsense. She loves you. Don't you love her?"

"I don't know! We've barely spent time together." James shook his head like he was dislodging something from it.

I felt myself getting frenzied. I had to think of something that would convince James to go through with this scheme so he could make up with Emily, but he glared back at me obstinately, his fists balled, his breathing coming a bit heavy. I grabbed James by the shoulders. "Listen to me," I began, but I was interrupted.

"I hope I'm not disturbing you," someone said gleefully. James and I turned and saw a beaming old woman approaching us. "You two looked so passionate, but you know, dinner is going to be served any moment now."

I released my grip on James's shoulders. "Oh, my apologies," I said. "I guess we had forgotten ourselves."

The old woman beamed even more, looking extremely pleased. "Don't worry yourselves about it.

How long have you been together, if you don't mind my asking?"

James began to wave his hands in front of himself and make noises. "We've been living together for about nine months," I told the old woman.

"Ohh!" she crowed. "Oh, oh, oh, oh! Oh my! You're living together, you say?" She looked at us a bit wistfully. "Good for you two. If I were young again, I would probably do the same." She then shoved off to dinner.

James looked at me and then broke into laughter. I began to laugh too. The tension that had arisen between us dissipated like so much mist. "James, you should go talk to Emily. It will be fine."

"Sure. And maybe I'll even try your crazy suggestion," he said. I raised my brows at him, but he pretended not to see. "You know, if I feel like it."

I nodded and gestured. "She's waiting for you over there. I need to leave now. Uncle Gerald is trying to make me meet with Robert Updike, and I'd like to avoid that."

I watched James walk over, say something to Emily, and move off with her. With the feeling of a job well done, I made for the front of the house, but as I was leaving the living room, I ran straight into Robert Updike himself. I say ran into him, but it was more like he pounced on me from behind a large chair.

"Ah ha!" he exclaimed.

I jumped about nine inches straight up. "Good heavens!" I exclaimed in turn.

"So, I've finally found you," he said. "We're going to need to have some words, you and I."

I gulped. My mind raced for a solution. I pointed out the window and shouted, "Is that the

Goodyear Blimp?"

There are times when your mind is humming along nicely and popping out fantastic idea after fantastic idea. And then there are times when it stutters and gives you what can only be described as a stinker. This fell firmly into the latter category, but as luck would have it, Robert Updike did not seem to be one of the best and brightest himself.

"What? Where?" he exclaimed, hurrying over to the window to have a look. I took the opportunity to make my escape and rushed to the back yard.

The back yard was the only place in the house which could accommodate a large group for dinner, and it was looking stuffed to the gills as people made their way there. Uncle Gerald had done this area up in grand style also, to give credit where credit is due. Gone were the wicker eggshells. Pink and white lanterns hung overhead from chords strung between the house and the fence. A long table complete with immaculate white linens dominated the scene, surrounded by a few smaller tables for those who were not afforded the honor of dining with my uncles. Servers were moving back and forth between the tables, making sure the guests had the drinks they required for dining. Scattered here and there were the tall space heaters which are ubiquitous at any outdoor gathering in Southern California.

I moved across the yard, trying to lose myself in the crowd, and stumbled across the table which it appeared my friends had been relegated to. James was sitting across from Emily, trying to look forlorn, but actually looking more like a kid on Christmas morning. Violet was talking animatedly at Emily. Travis was nowhere to been seen, which somehow worried me.

Violet waved at me. "Haverford, you look like you've seen a ghost."

"I'm being pursued by Robert Updike," I informed her. "I gave him the slip with the old Goodyear Blimp trick, but I need to get out of here before he catches up with me."

Emily and James both looked at me wide-eyed. "Like in Bill and Ted?" they said in unison. "Oh!" they said in unison again, and then looked at each other with surprise.

"You're hiding from Uncle Bobby?" Violet asked. "Did you know I had a chance to talk to him? You don't need to worry about the letter anymore."

I laughed bitterly. "No, I don't need to worry about that, but I've heard from Uncle Gerald that he wants to give me a job, provided I apologize."

"So then don't apologize," Violet said. "Not that it would be the worst thing for you to work at Tompkins, Richards, and Armstrong. But if you're so dead set against it, Uncle Bobby is right there behind that space heater. Just go tell him you're not sorry for what you did."

The idea Violet proposed struck me as absolute madness. To march into the lion's den, as it were, and tell him off straight to his face? I was about to explain why I would never do that, but James suddenly jumped into the conversation.

"I don't know why these space heaters are here," James said. "It's over seventy degrees right now, isn't it?"

"Oh, just one of those idiosyncrasies those who were born in Southern California adore," I said, getting distracted. "Violet used to make quite a fuss about it when we first met." I turned to her. "Violet, do you remember what it was you said on those occasions? It was something extremely amusing about layering jackets, as I recall."

Violet rolled her eyes at me. "I said people in Southern California should learn how to layer. Maybe wear a light jacket in the evening."

"You see? She really has a gift for comedy."

"Layering actually is a good idea, Cecil," James said, looking thoughtful. "It really doesn't seem like anyone here does know how to layer."

"James, please," I gasped with laughter. "I'd love to stick around being entertained by all this vaudeville, but I really need to make myself scarce."

Before anyone could say more, Travis arrived and dropped a chair laden with a full place setting on the ground. "'Sup guys," he said. "I'm just helping my new best bro Earl move to our table." He gestured to the old man he had been talking to earlier, who was hobbling his way towards us with something approaching alacrity.

I saw what Travis was doing. He used to call me his best bro, and so by calling Earl his best bro, he was implying that I had lost that status. It was a transparent move to make me jealous, and after congratulating myself on spotting it I raised my eyebrows and said "I'm not sure if that's allowed. Uncle Gerald is very strict about his seating arrangements."

Violet, however, appeared to want to have fun. "Now, I thought Haverford here was your best friend," she said, doing an absolutely awful job at registering shock and alarm at what she had just heard. "Has something happened between you two?"

"Well, you know how it is with bros," Travis

said, waving a philosophical hand. "It's like, stuff happens, or whatever."

"No, I really don't know," Violet said. "Please, if you wouldn't mind telling us."

"How long have you known this guy?" James interrupted while defending his plate from Earl, who was trying to place it with the rest of the dishes on his chair.

"I totally get it, James, bro," Travis said, patting James's shoulder. "You're like, oh man, why am I not Travis's best bro now? I've known him longer. All I can say about that is it's like, opportunity, you know? Your best bro is the guy who's there for you when you need him." Travis glared at me. "Right? Your best bro is there for you when you need him," he enunciated each word. "Earl here took one of those little cocktail wieners out to Turkey. Boom, instant best bro."

I believe I gasped aloud in surprise. "You didn't bring Turkey, did you? Travis, this is a fancy party! You simply cannot bring a dog here."

"It's cool, he's waiting in the car. I'm not gonna, like, insist he has a seat at the table. He's not gonna dance or steal someone's girlfriend."

I had a burning retort on the tip of my tongue, but before I could unleash it Uncle Gerald entered our conversation with a splash. "Thank you all for joining us," he said to the table. "It is a pleasure to have you all here. Won't you join me in a toast to celebrate my nephew receiving a position at Tompkins, Richards, and Armstrong? We're so very proud of him finally being able to make his own way in the world."

I once again gasped in shock. "Uncle Gerald, whatever do you mean?" I said. "That wasn't supposed to be worked out until I spoke to Robert Updike, and

I haven't done that yet."

Uncle Gerald looked at me imperiously. "But I have," he said.

Robert Updike approached just then. "Perhaps I should clarify," he began, but Uncle Gerald shut him down with a hard look.

"You are employed," he stated simply to me. "You will have means with which to support yourself. Your upkeep is now your own concern."

"But how on earth did this happen?" I said. "I have not earned this position! You already know about how my interview went, and the letter I sent to him."

"Well, you see, it is actually conditional—" Robert Updike attempted to interject again.

Uncle Gerald let loose with a noise that sounded like, "Tchah," and then his mouth snapped shut and compressed down to a straight line. "I recall all of your failures," he unclamped to say. "But I have worked it out with Bob. He wants to hire you, pending one final short interview which will happen here, under my supervision."

"If I may," Robert Updike said forcefully enough to dislodge Uncle Gerald's vice grip on the conversation. "As I said, it is conditional on young Mr. Haverford here assisting me in a matter."

Uncle Gerald flung his hands skyward. "Oh, very well," he said.

Robert Updike made a noise in his throat, apparently to prepare for speaking a great deal. "Once a year we do team building at Tompkins, Richards, and Armstrong. Last year some of the younger staff members lobbied for the team building exercise to include playing a racing video game." Robert Updike paused as a look of pain passed over his face. "I came in last in every race. I was the laughingstock of the office."

An awkward silence descended on our group as Robert Updike grappled with his personal sorrow. "There, there," James said, causing Robert Updike to recall himself.

"That won't happen this year," he continued. "I've learned from my niece, Miss Andrews, that you, sir," he pointed at me, "possess knowledge of something called a 'banana trick' which will ensure my victory."

I was baffled. "So you want me to teach you the banana trick," I said.

Robert Updike nodded. "Yes, and in return you may have the job you interviewed for."

"That's not fair!" James cried. "It goes against standards of ethics."

"Ethics be damned! I must have the banana trick!"

"But there is no banana trick," I said. "It was just beginner's luck. Violet knows that."

"Ha!" Violet exclaimed, and then she did it again for good measure. "Ha! I knew it! And now I've got you to admit it."

Travis looked shocked. "Vi, say that's not the truth. I know the banana trick exists."

"I agree with that young man," Robert Updike said. "Tell me the banana trick and you'll get that job."

Something about the plain and simple way he put it spurred me into action. I had no secret to tell, and I did not want that job, so my response was instant and definite. "Absolutely not!" I shouted, leaping onto the table. "I will not take your job, I'm not sorry for sending you a love letter or throwing up on you, and I don't like your tie."

This caused a general commotion to erupt. James started in again on Robert Updike about workplace ethics, while Violet and Travis argued about banana tricks. Emily was clutching at her head, clearly in some amount of pain. I, in my rage, had begun hurling dishware on the ground, assisted by Earl, who kept handing things up to me.

Uncle Gerald wasn't about to lose control of his own party, though. He roared above the hubbub, "John Haverford, get down from that table this instant!"

You would have expected my friends to react to Uncle Gerald revealing my first name. It would only be right to see strong men faint and strong women leap about in response to such a bombshell. And perhaps, once the initial shock wore off, that would have been the case. This we will never know, because at that moment another disturbance caught everyone's attention. There was a clattering and crashing noise from across the yard, and then I saw Washington Irving, or a cat very much like him, with Turkey hot on his heels.

CHAPTER 16

I have perhaps done Turkey a disservice by not describing him in detail before, so I will attempt to fix that now. Turkey is an American Bulldog, which means that he is rather broad and stocky. He retains the flat snout and severe under-bite of an English Bulldog, while most others of his breed have a longer snout and what, if my resources are correct, is referred to as a "reverse scissors" bite, whatever that means. He is mostly white, with a black patch over one eye and a black tail. The most notable thing about Turkey is his size. Whereas most American Bulldogs will top out at 120 pounds, Travis had somehow raised his dog to a whopping 145 pounds of muscle. Bulldogs were originally bred to fight bulls, I hear, and Turkey would make any bull think twice about tangling with him.

Not that he was vicious. In fact, as a general rule, you couldn't find a sweeter companion. That is, until a cat showed up. Turkey is not one of those who finds the stereotype of dogs chasing cats laughably quaint. When faced with any sort of feline, he gets a head full of steam and rushes towards it. He has yet to catch a cat, probably because they are all smarter than him, but he does enjoy the chase.

When you take a dog with the size and temperament of Turkey and a cat who may or may not be Washington Irving and turn them loose at a dinner party hosted by my Uncle Gerald, what you get is nothing less than pandemonium. Turkey did a remarkably good job keeping up in this instance, being big and determined enough to run through nearly all obstacles. No matter how the cat zigged and zagged, Turkey was just behind, knocking over chairs and causing people to jump out of his way.

Washington Irving found his way to our table, ran across it, hopped on Uncle Gerald's shoulders, and clung there, hissing like he had sprung a leak. Turkey, owing to the remarkable agility and jumping ability of his breed, also leapt on the table, knocking me to the ground. He appeared ready to jump on Uncle Gerald also, but one fierce look made him stop in his tracks. Knowing when he was beaten, Turkey tucked his tail between his legs and scurried back into the house.

I stood up, brushed myself off, and surveyed the scene. The dinner party had certainly become untidy, to say the least. Guests were clustered in small groups. I heard the nearest group discussing, with no small amount of animation, how it was the most exciting dinner party they had been to this year. I noticed Travis was no longer among us, and I spotted him dashing towards the house with Earl on his back. James and Violet were clustered around Emily, who was looking decidedly worse for the wear. I approached them.

"Well, you can't say this is a dull party, can

you?" I said conversationally.

"Oh, it's Cecil," Emily said. "Or is it John? Are you a secret agent spy sent to gather government secrets?" For a moment a whimsical light shone in her eyes, then she grimaced and rubbed her head.

"But really, what's the deal with that?" James asked. "Did you change your name or something?"

"Cecil is his middle name," Violet answered. She paused, as if unsure whether she wanted to say more. "He decided he needed to be fancy."

"Not fancy," I said. "It was for my career. No one will buy books from someone named John. But a Cecil Haverford, how could anyone pass that up?"

"He started talking with that affected tone around the same time he started going by Cecil," Violet said. She gave me a look. "It was soon after your parents passed away, wasn't it?"

I felt my face grow hot. This was not something I wanted to talk about at the moment. "Never mind about that," I said, annoyed.

"It doesn't matter if it's John or Cecil," James said. "You're still, well, you know. You're definitely unique."

"Thank you, James," I said. "Putting that to the side, I think the party is more or less over now. Shall we take our leave?"

"Excuse me, but you're not going anywhere," Uncle Gerald said. I jumped in spite of myself. I had completely forgotten that Uncle Gerald was there.

"Why, Uncle Gerald. Lovely party. I am afraid I will be needing to leave, however."

Uncle Gerald ignored my words. "John Haverford," he began, using my full name to indicate his displeasure.

"Now listen," I interrupted him. "If I've told you once, I've told you a thousand times, please call me Cecil now."

"I'll call you whatever I please. Now you will go find that mutt and restrain it."

"Now, now, Gerald," Uncle Ted said. "I don't know if we need to do anything to that critter. He's just following his nature."

I was quick to voice my agreement. "Uncle Ted is right. I can assure you that Turkey is completely harmless to people. He merely dislikes cats."

"Harmless?" Uncle Gerald shrieked. "Look at what that creature has done! Do you know what it takes to put on an event like this?"

I admitted that the party was certainly in shambles, and the inconvenience to Uncle Gerald was significant. Still, I felt that Turkey shouldn't be punished excessively. "What are you going to do with him?" I asked.

Uncle Gerald breathed in, and I could tell he was carefully considering what to say. "I will do nothing to the animal," he decided. "You are right, it is an animal. But someone must own that animal, and I intend to hold it until that person steps forward and takes responsibility for this." He looked at Uncle Ted, who was scratching Washington Irving under the chin. "Put him down!" he snapped. He turned back to me. "You find that dog and bring it to me."

When Uncle Gerald uses that tone, the discussion is at an end. Mine was no longer to reason why, mine was now to do and die. I walked towards the house, feeling rather shaken. I didn't even notice Uncle Ted was walking with me until he spoke.

"Listen, John," he started. I reminded him it

was Cecil now, but he brushed it aside. "You find that dog and get him out of here."

I nodded. "Yes, that was my plan."

Uncle Ted looked satisfied. "Well good. I'll calm Gerald down. He's more sensitive than he lets on, you know, and that frisky little critter put a fright in him."

I considered reminding him just how large Turkey was, but I decided there was no point with Uncle Ted. "Thank you, Uncle Ted," I told him instead.

Uncle Ted gripped my shoulders, and I fancied I saw a tear or two in his eyes. "Cecil, I'm very proud of you. You can do anything."

"Yes, yes, absolutely."

"You just have to be willing to pay the price for it."

"Undoubtedly."

"Nothing is beyond your grasp, you hear me?"

"Loud and clear, old chum."

Uncle Ted attempted to ruffle my hair, but I ducked away. "Go get 'em!" he said as I trotted to the house.

You would think that finding one rather large dog in a house would be no problem, but I confess I found the task to be absolutely impossible. I looked high and low for some minutes, finding nothing. Finally, I located Travis in one of the guest rooms. I felt confident that he would have some information on where Turkey might be hiding.

"Travis, Uncle Gerald is looking for Turkey. Where is he?"

Travis threw me against a wall and raised a fist. "Don't you dare, bro. You're not putting a finger on

Turkey. I heard him. He's gonna put him down. Forget that, man. No one's finding Turkey."

I was puzzled for a moment. It didn't seem like Uncle Gerald had said that at all. Then I saw what had happened. Travis had heard Uncle Gerald tell Uncle Ted to put down Washington Irving, and thought he was talking about Turkey. "Allow me to explain," I began.

"I don't think so. I heard your uncles, dude. Just back off and no one has to get hurt."

"Travis, I swear, I'm trying to help Turkey. Uncle Ted is too. He loves all animals because a man on TV named Bob Ross told him to."

"Dude, that's like, the oldest trick in the book. Bob Ross is such a lame name. That's like two first names. I'm not falling for any of that grade school stuff."

"Travis, again I must assure you that there is no trickery happening here." I placed a hand on his massive arm. "I love Turkey, okay? I love him. He's the best dog I ever met. I would sooner never receive a cent from my uncles again than let anything happen to him. Believe me, I am trying to save Turkey."

Travis looked at me for a moment, then tears welled up in his eyes and he grabbed me in a painful bear hug. "I'm so scared, bro!" he cried. "I heard your uncle say that, and I can't lose Turkey!"

"It will be fine, I promise," I said, awkwardly patting his back. "He was talking about the cat, and in a different way than you think." I wriggled out of his grasp. "But there is some trouble. He wants to hold Turkey's owner responsible for the damage, and that's you. He's planning on caging Turkey until you step forward. So we need to get both of you out of here.

Now, do you know where Turkey might have gone?"

Travis wiped at his eyes. "Oh yeah, no worries there. I found him and put him in hiding. Earl is guarding him."

"Earl? That old man?" I wiped my brow, thinking at this moment he was probably doing something ridiculous like putting flowers on Turkey's head. "No, this is a terrible plan."

"No way, it's great. Dude used to be like a Karate fighter in the war or something."

I rubbed my head, feeling a bit of an ache coming on, and had a momentary thought of compassion towards Violet. How could she… but I let it go. "Let's just collect Turkey and get out of here." Travis nodded in agreement and as we were about to move, we heard Uncle Gerald issuing orders to some unseen persons.

"Watch the exits. Make sure no one leaves with that dog. We'll flush it out of hiding…" He was moving and the rest of what he said was indistinct. Travis and I exchanged worried glances.

"Dude, I think we're boned."

"We can't give up yet. One of us will have to run interference while the other sneaks Turkey out."

"Okay, bro, I'll do the interference part. You go get Turkey. I stashed him in a closet." Travis then pulled me in for another bear hug. "I'm sorry, dude. You really are my best bro, and you always will be." He released me, tore off his jacket and shirt, and sprang down the hall. "Who's up for keg-stands?" he bellowed.

"Wait, Travis! Which closet?" I called after him, but he was gone. I did a quick search of the closet in the bedroom, but Turkey was nowhere to be seen.

As I rushed out of the room, I felt so frustrated I could have uttered a curse word.

"Haverford, there you are," someone said behind me.

"Shi—" I gasped as I whirled around and saw Violet. "Shift! Shifty business. Is what this clearly is. Violet, where did you spring from?"

"I've been looking for Turkey. What are you doing up here?"

"I'm also looking for Turkey. I found Travis, and apparently he's secreted the pooch away somewhere. He just left to run interference so I can get Turkey out of here."

"Is that what he was doing?" Violet laughed. "I saw him giving a lap dance to someone's grandma." A certain look came into her eyes, then she seemed to recall herself. "What do we know about Turkey's location?"

"He's in a closet somewhere, but Travis didn't mention the exact location."

"Very well. I'll look up here, you go downstairs." Violet paused. "I'm sorry I brought up your parents. I know that's a sensitive subject for you."

I gazed at the floor. "I appreciate you saying that."

"I do wish you would talk to someone about it. I think you bottling up your feelings is having a really negative effect. I care for you, you know."

I was taken aback. "You can't mean that. What about Travis? I don't pretend to understand that situation, but surely—"

"I don't mean it like that," she said. "I care for you as a friend and fellow human being."

I nodded, suddenly feeling the weight of grief

I had never managed to express. I pushed it aside as best I could. "Maybe I'll talk to you about it later, when we aren't trying to find a dog to protect a friend from the burden of a fiscal responsibility he cannot hope to bear."

"Do you think your uncle will try to make him pay damages?"

"Undoubtedly. Uncle Gerald is fierce, and his party was ruined."

"Then like you said, let's help him avoid responsibility."

I turned to leave, then turned back. "What is the deal with you two, anyway?"

Violet looked at me with her composed eyes. "He's the man I'm going to marry," she said, cool as anything.

I shook my head in bewilderment, not sure if she was joking, and rushed downstairs. At the foot of the stairs, James suddenly appeared before me. "Cecil, I need to talk to you."

"Certainly, my good man. I have nothing but free time at the moment. For instance, I am not attempting to find a dog."

James blinked at me with his mouth open. "What are you talking about?"

"Never mind. How are you and Emily doing?"

"I think the mood is spoiled," he said. "Have you ever seen such a mess?"

"Hm, how unfortunate. But I don't have time to commiserate. If you see Turkey, let me know. He's most likely in a closet."

I left James and went to the entryway. I decided that was a good place to start looking. The entry closet was around a corner from my perspective, near the front door. I moved towards it and bumped into Emily.

I felt ambivalent about this. On the one hand there was my renewed attraction for Emily, which was a force not to be discounted. On the other hand, I was trying to find Turkey and get him out of here, and I kept being interrupted and distracted. And on the other, other hand, there was James to consider. Still, I felt it wouldn't do to just stand there gawking at her.

"Hello, Emily," I said cordially.

"Oh, Cecil," she said distantly. "I was just leaving. I think the party is over anyway, and I really need to get some rest."

"Indeed. Well, safe travels and all that."

"Thank you, maybe I'll see you soon." She moved towards me and gave me a gentle hug.

I felt everything crystallize at that moment. Or maybe it was the stress of the evening causing me to react. Either way, I found myself on one knee, clasping Emily's hand in the way which suggests burning passion.

"Emily let's leave this place together," I said in my most throbbing voice. "Let's roll on the beach together and share a sundae and have babies. I can't bear to be apart anymore. It doesn't matter if you want to be a college professor or worse, even a dean. I am madly in love with you!"

Emily had been trying to interrupt me as I spoke, and she finally wedged her way between my words. "Stop Cecil, that's too much! I can't believe you!"

"Why not? Our lives can be like a movie from this point on. Isn't that the kind of thing you want?"

"No, Cecil, it's not. You have no idea what I

want."

"It's James, isn't it? I get it. He's the boring sap, you're the spunky lady, and you're going to change his life for the better."

"Shut up!" she exploded. "Stop implying I'm one of those manic pixie girls. I like James just how he is. He's sweet and funny and easy going, and he's great."

"Is that true, Emily?" James asked. Emily made a squeaking noise and covered her face. I felt equally embarrassed and decided it was time for me to leave. I backed up, felt behind me for a doorknob, turned it, and staggered forward as something shoved the door open.

"Oh no, Turkey!" I exclaimed. I had inadvertently opened the closet in the entryway, and Turkey came bounding out, happy as a clam. I tried to push him back in, but as I did someone grabbed me from behind, spun me roughly around, and punched me in the face.

I have since researched the science of punching, and I am confident that I was struck with a type of punch called a hook. It is performed, as near as I can tell, as follows: bend your arm to create a 90-degree angle at the elbow. Step in with the opposite foot of the bent arm, then pivot your body and raise the bent arm to be roughly parallel with the floor. The pivoting motion is what creates the force behind the punch. It takes a bit of practice, but the results, as I can attest, are devastating.

The force of the punch spun me clear around in a circle. Somehow, I stayed upright despite the wobbling of my legs and the feeling of my head revolving on its axis. I saw Earl shaking out his right hand and dancing a jig. Emily was looking at me in shock, while James reached out to steady me. He was too late, however, and I felt myself slide down and hit my head on something. The last thing I remember thinking was that Travis was right. Earl was one heck of a Karate fighter.

CHAPTER 17

I woke up in my bed. I felt disoriented and confused, and I was even more so when I saw Robert Updike filling the chair next to me.

"Excuse me for interrupting you at your home," he said. "I know you've just suffered a trauma." He indicated at my face. I felt my left eye, which was tender to the touch and swollen almost shut. I would probably have a black eye for some time.

"Ah yes," I said. I expected to feel my nerves jangle at the sight of him, but there was a strange calm instead. I've read that those who have faced deadly peril and come through intact will sometimes react in this way. Staring their own mortality in the face gives them the perspective to see that the Robert Updikes of the world are only a minor inconvenience that will not impede their desire to live a good life. Having been punched by an elderly gentleman, I was experiencing this firsthand.

While I was entertaining these thoughts, Robert Updike sat in my chair, nervously fidgeting with his tie. I couldn't understand what he was doing in my room, and I decided I needed to get to the bottom of this mystery.

"To what do I owe this pleasure?" I asked, surprised at how cold my voice sounded. Here was a man who not a day ago would have turned me to a pillar of salt with one glower, and now I was speaking to him as if I were Uncle Gerald.

It reminded me of a time from my childhood, when I got cast in my elementary school play for the titular role of the Self-Esteem Robbing Dragon, or SERD to his friends. At our first dress rehearsal I was nervous, a shrinking violet if you will, and when I spoke, I was barely audible. Those in charge decided to fit me with a microphone, however come performance time the microphone did not work. I miraculously rose to the occasion though, delivering my lines with a clarity and volume that no one had suspected me of possessing.

"State your business," I said with the self-possession of SERD.

Robert Updike had moved from fidgeting with his tie to rubbing his palms against his thighs. "I'll be brief. I lost track of you in the fracas last night, so we couldn't finish our conversation. I'm here to discuss the job offer with you."

I nodded. This was to be expected, and so I had an answer ready for him. "I'm afraid I have to decline. I am a writer, you see, and not suited for the life of working at a law firm." I had a sudden thought. "But why am I even being offered this job? It can't be because you think I'm qualified, and I'm certain that I did not wow you at any point in our interactions."

"Oh no, my boy, no, no, no." Robert Updike

laughed uproariously. "After last night you wouldn't possibly be offered a job at Tompkins, Richards, and Armstrong. Too volatile. You're not even remotely TRA material." He chuckled again and resumed rubbing his palms against his thighs. "No, I'm here about the services you can provide me."

I couldn't possibly see where he was going with this, so I just stared blankly.

He stopped rubbing his palms against his thighs and began flexing his fingers. I was beginning to feel annoyed at his fidgeting. "Surely you remember," he said. "That racing video game. How I will be the laughingstock of the office."

"You don't say?" I said politely.

"Oh yes, absolutely. You can't imagine the savagery of a law firm when they smell weakness. To state my case again, my niece Violet says you have information on a trick to win, a banana trick she called it, and I want it. I can't offer you that job anymore, but I'm sure we can come to some mutually beneficial arrangement."

For a moment I had a vision of soaking this poor corpulent serpent for all he was worth. I wondered how much I could get out of him. But there were two problems. First was that I still had no idea what the banana trick was, if it even existed. Second was that I did not want to spend any time in Robert Updike's presence.

"I am afraid, sir, that I must disappoint you," I said in my most grim, foreboding manner.

Robert Updike turned purple on hearing this. "You are refusing my offer?"

I nodded resolutely. "I am."

"But what about my reputation?" he asked,

trying to appeal to my softer feelings. "How can I come back from being a laughingstock a second time?"

I shook my head at him. His jaw firmed up.

"I will pay you forty dollars an hour for your lessons," he said, appealing to my greed now.

I admit I wavered. Forty dollars is not enough to shake me to my core, but if I did not waver, I would not be human. Still I was able to hold firm. "It will not happen."

He stood and did his best to majestically sweep from the room, but he caught his foot on the chair he had been sitting in and stumbled. He opened the door and paused before exiting. "You will rue this," he said, and on that line he exited as if he were leaving the stage in a play.

The air whooshed out of me, but no sooner had I fallen back in relief when Uncle Ted walked in.

"Well, I'll be," he said and emitted a piercing whistle of admiration. "That's a fine shiner you've got there, Cecil."

"Thank you, Uncle Ted," I said with grace. "Please come in."

Uncle Ted shuffled his feet. "Well, actually, it's not just me," he admitted, and Uncle Gerald stepped into the doorway from wherever he had been lurking. I shot an accusatory glance at Uncle Ted.

"Well, John," Uncle Gerald said, and looked at me haughtily. I stared back. Uncle Gerald began to swell a bit like a frog about to have an apoplexy, if that's the word to use when you mean to say the frog in question, or uncle as the case may be, is ready to explode. "I'd like to apologize," he finally managed.

The room spun about me as if I had just stepped from a poorly managed carnival ride. "Do my ears deceive me?" I gasped. "This is a world first! Uncle Ted, I'm glad you're here to witness this."

"Oh shut up," Uncle Gerald snapped. "Let me just get this over with so I can leave. We have a dinner to attend tonight." I glanced over their clothing and felt convinced that they were doing something fancy somewhere.

"Please, Uncle Gerald, come in."

He nodded, entered, and perched himself on the chair Robert Updike had recently vacated. I watched him prepare for a moment, and then he launched into it like one of those people in the northern parts of the world who leap into freezing lakes for fun. "I'm afraid I may have caused you some embarrassment last night."

I remained on my guard. I wasn't sure which embarrassment he was referring to, and thought a measured silence was my best bet.

Uncle Gerald hesitated, expecting some sort of response. When it was clear he wouldn't get one, he continued. "I said that Bob Updike was offering you a job at Tompkins, Richards, and Armstrong, but it seems I was mistaken. So, I apologize." He nearly didn't make it, his voice squeaking on the word apologize. He cleared his throat and continued. "I fear you may have been relying on that job, so I've decided to continue your allowance until such a time as I am able to find you another opportunity."

"I appreciate that, Uncle Gerald. In the spirit of sharing I should let you know that Robert Updike did in fact offer me a job as his private tutor." I braced myself for the reaction this next bit would provoke. "I just turned him down."

Uncle Gerald's lips compressed. "Why?" he

asked.

"Frankly, I couldn't bear to be in his presence any longer."

Uncle Gerald nodded. "He is not the most pleasant person. I would never recommend you to a position directly under him. Your decision is acceptable. My offer still stands."

Uncle Ted slapped me on the back and said "That's great, Cecil! I'm proud of you. Integrity is invaluable."

"I would still like you to have employment," Uncle Gerald told me. "But I recognize that I should go about it differently. What sort of work interests you?"

"Uncle Gerald, you know I am a writer."

He sighed. "Yes, I know. Your parents had such faith in you about that. I'm afraid I want a more assured success for you. I care for you dearly, but I can't be like them."

I felt the feeling of grief rise in me again, but this time I didn't push it away. I shed a tear. "I do miss them. But I don't know why you think you need to be like them."

"Someone needs to look after you. How on earth will you manage?"

"But I'm not a child anymore!"

"I've got it!" Uncle Ted declared, bopping his fist onto his open palm. "John, you still need our financial support in order to not live in squalor. But you shouldn't just be given it for free. You should have to earn it in some way. So, we'll be your patrons, and in a year's time you will produce a book. How does that sound?"

I thought it was a fantastic idea and said so.

Uncle Gerald had some reservations but agreed. "It's better than you continuing to fritter away your time doing nothing," he said.

"I won't fail," I promised them. I still felt a lump in my throat from earlier, and I felt compelled to say more. "I don't express this often enough, but I do love you both."

Uncle Gerald looked surprised and embarrassed. "I love you too," he said hastily. "See that you succeed."

Uncle Ted just beamed at me, and then they left, closing the door after them. I settled back in bed and had just started marveling at the twists of life when my door opened again, and James and Emily popped in.

"You're awake," James said. "I mean, I assumed you would be with everyone coming to see you, but it's nice that you're awake."

I nodded at him. "Oh yes, it's quite nice for me as well." I suddenly realized I had no idea how I got home or what had happened the previous night. I was too caught up with Robert Updike and my uncles to give it any thought. "James, what in the world happened last night? Is Turkey okay? What about Travis?"

"You don't remember?" James asked.

"It was a nasty bump you got," Emily said. "Not to mention getting punched in the face. It doesn't really look good."

"It's not great, but it will improve. But what happened?"

James rubbed the back of his neck. "Well, you got hit and fell down. Then Turkey was on the loose. He went for Emily, and it turns out she's afraid of dogs."

"Especially ones that look like that!" Emily exclaimed. "But then James was like a dog whisperer and calmed him."

"I told him to stay," James explained. "I know how obedient he is. Travis has done well with him."

"You were wonderful! Then, Cecil, your uncle showed up and demanded to know if that dog belonged to James."

"And what did you say?" I asked, feeling on the edge of my seat, were I actually seated and not lying down.

"I said no."

I nodded. "Smart move, since he isn't. What then?"

"He said he would cage the dog until the owner stepped forward."

"Right, he had told me he would do that. Nice to see him being consistent."

"Travis did step forward, though," Emily said. "But he didn't say he owned the dog, and he was only wearing gold underwear."

I gasped. "You're pulling my leg. I told him to cause a distraction, but that seems just silly."

"It's true," James said.

"What did he do then?" I asked.

James looked uncomfortable. "I'd rather not talk about it."

I looked to Emily, but she just shook her head, wide-eyed.

James cleared his throat. "Anyway, when order had been restored, you and Turkey were both gone. That's why I thought you must have remembered something. Then your uncle kicked us all out of his house."

"So where did we go?" I asked.

"Turkey wound up in Travis's car," James said. "Your car was gone, and we didn't know where you were until I got home and found you asleep in bed."

I breathed a sigh of relief. It seemed that even when I was unconscious, my mind could still keep going. No doubt I somehow sensed the group as a whole was distracted and took that opportunity to sneak Turkey out from under everyone's collective noses. I suddenly quivered with shock and surprise. "Are you suggesting that I drove myself to San Diego while unconscious?" I asked.

Emily shrugged. "Maybe you did wake up and you just don't remember anything. I think that kind of thing can happen."

As she said that I suddenly remembered how I had spoken to her the night before. "Emily, I do have to apologize for what I said."

She smiled. "It's okay, I'm sure after that bump you weren't thinking clearly."

"But I said that before—" I began, but Emily shot me a look which made me stop. I understood. James is a sensitive soul who would not take it well if he knew I had confessed my feelings to Emily in such a way. "Say, are you two actually dating?" I asked.

James looked embarrassed and began stammering something, but Emily grabbed his arm and silenced him. "We are. He's absolutely wonderful, and did you know he just got a new job? He won't be working at The Pet Store anymore, and this law firm he'll be working at is a really big deal."

"James, that's wonderful!" I congratulated him. "Where is this job at?"

"Oh, it's that place we interviewed at, Tompkins, Richards, and Armstrong."

"You don't say! So they hand-picked you out of that crop that was there? Well, I understand why."

"I suppose so," he said sheepishly. "I just found out now. But it's not the job I interviewed for."

"So why did you take it?" I asked, confused.

"There are more advancement opportunities."

I was about to question whether advancement opportunities would be sufficiently fulfilling, when suddenly Violet, Travis, and Turkey entered. "Haverford, I've been worried sick!" Violet yelled at me. "You can't just vanish when you have a head trauma."

"I had no idea what I was doing," I said. "Where did you all come from?"

Violet scowled at me. "We were hiding in James's room. Your uncle came over, and we thought it best he didn't see Travis or Turkey. He never figured out whose dog it was, and we intend to keep it that way."

Travis came over and practically lifted me out of bed in a giant hug. "Bro, you totally saved Turkey again. I knew you were my best bro!"

"Again? What was the first time?" I asked.

"You still don't remember? I guess your brain is all scrambled right now, so it's cool. It was when we met." He looked at James and Emily. "Have you heard about this? I was at the beach, doing my thing, surfing with Turkey and stuff. He was on this little wimpy wave—" Turkey barked at Travis here, as if objecting. "Bro, it was totally a weak-sauce wave. Anyway, he bails and I'm like nowhere near and not paying attention really because I thought there's no way he'd fall off that one. He was in totally serious danger of drowning, because bulldogs can't get their heads out of the water."

"Are you saying Cecil jumped into the water to save him?" James asked.

"Nah, he pointed it out to a lifeguard who saved Turkey. But if he wasn't there, I'm sure that lifeguard wouldn't have done squat."

I gaped at Travis. "I thought that was a child," I said. "I had no idea it was Turkey." I turned to the others. "I could not for the life of me figure out why this guy and his dog followed me home afterwards. To think that was Turkey." I patted him on the head, then Travis joined me, and soon we were giving Turkey all the attention a dog could ask for.

When everyone had left, I was lying in bed pondering how things can sometimes turn out. I snuggled down, feeling the need for some more rest, but just as I was falling asleep my door burst open again and Travis leapt into the middle of the room.

"Dude, bro!" he said excitedly. "Guess who just asked Violet out on a date? I totally crushed it! Gimme some!" He extended his hand for a fist bump.

"Travis, I can hear you," Violet said from the living room. "I'm right here."

NOTE FROM THE AUTHOR

Thank you for reading! As an independent author, reviews help spread the word. Please consider reviewing this book on my Amazon.com author page: www.amazon.com/author/rhyswolfe

Made in the USA
Middletown, DE
03 January 2020

82495077R00106